Modern Midrashim

*a fusion of modern short stories
with ancient traditions*

Rabbi Lenny Sarko

To JOAN

with All [...]

Modern Midrashim

*a fusion of modern short stories
with ancient traditions*

First Edition

*ISBN: 978-0-578-06088-0
LCCN: 2010930672*

*Printed in the USA by
Instantpublisher.com*

Table of Contents

Leviticus

Numbers

Deuteronomy

Illustrators

The listings under each illustrator are by Midrash title.

Regina Befera:
Vaera, Beshalach, Mishpatim, Terumah, Ki Tisa, Vayikra, Shemini, Tazria, Metzora, Kedoshim, Bechukosai, Bamidbar, Nasso, Beha'aloscha, Shelach, Korach, Chukat, Mattot, Devarim, Re'eh, Ki Teitzei, Vayeilech, Haazinu, Vezot Haberachah

Carolyn Garay:
Yito

Troy Palmer-Hughes:
Shemot, Tetzaveh, Tzav, Behar, Masei, Eikev, Ki Tavo, Nitzavim

Ross J. Slater-Finch:
Pekudei, Emor, Shoftim

Melanie Stephens:
Bo, Vayakhel, Acharei, Balak, Va'eschanan

Andrew Ward:
Bereshit, Noach, Lech Lecha, Vayeira, Cayei Sarah, Toldot, Vayeitzei, Vayishlach, Vayeishev, Mikeitz, Vayigash, Vaychi

Acknowledgments

I wanted to first thank the six illustrators for their contribution to this book. Their vision added a new dimension which the readers I am sure will appreciate.

There have been many people that helped edit this text. Although their names are not mentioned, please know how much I appreciated your comments and how much help they were in the composition of this work.

I wanted to give extra special mention to my son, Michael Sarko, whose editorial assistance was invaluable. His professional critique helped polish this work and kept me focused. I am indebted to him for his backing, support and expertise.

Dedication

To Karen
My wife, my companion, my beshert

Introduction

Midrash is a method used for investigation and interpretation of a verse in the Five Books of Moses. It is designed to teach a Judaic lesson through the form of a story. Many Midrashim (plural of Midrash) were committed to writing between the 2nd and 11th centuries, although this literary form has been found throughout Jewish history.

The stories found in this book reflect the ancient tradition of the Midrashim. The purpose of these stories is to relate some lesson that may be found as part of the Five Books of Moses. I have chosen to use modern setting for these stories in part to relate that the lessons found within the Bible are still current, important and applicable. I believe that in using modern settings it allows the reader to better relate the lesson to be learned.

These stories are divided by Parasha. The Five Books of Moses were divided into weekly segments or Parshiot (plural). There are fifty-four Parshiot in the Jewish Bible. One Parasha is recited weekly in the synagogue. That same Parasha is defined and recited, based on the specific week of the calendar, in every congregation throughout the world. So the Parasha for a specific week is the same whether in Argentina, France, Australia or the United States. If a person walks into any synagogue in the world for that date, they will hear the same Biblical portion. It is a way the Jewish community is connected regardless of location.

For each story one concept was gleaned from the titled Parasha and a story developed to help explain my interpretation of that concept from the Biblical portion. Judaism is not a simple religion. It forces us to think, analyze and interpret. Judaism believes in brit- covenant. We have a partnership with God. As such we need to participate in its development and application.

Our different understandings cause us to talk, to discuss, to debate. I hope that these stories will spur such discussion, and promote such dialogue. To do so will best reflect the intent of the method of Midrashim.

Shalom b'shalom,
Farewell in peace,

Rabbi Lenny Sarko

Midrash Bereshit
Creation

It was a small college, in the middle of a small town, in the middle of Middle America, and Jeff was the best architect to ever grace its halls. He wanted to do something special for the years of loyalty that the school and the local people bestowed on him. He decided to build a memorial on the college campus. Jeff presented it to the college and the town. He would not only finance and purchase all the required materials at no cost to the college or city, but design and build the memorial himself. They agreed.

For weeks Jeff struggled with what to build and then it dawned on him. It came together like the inspiration of creation blossoming in the midst of a void. He began to collect the materials.

The first thing Jeff did was to set up lights all around the selected area. It took him all evening and all morning to set the poles and lights where he wanted. He set up a tent to conceal the work from people poking around- the first day.

A few people gathered around the tent to see what Jeff was doing. The second day Jeff brought cloud looking structures into the tent and extended a water hose from a hydrant to inside the tent- the second day.

On the third day Jeff dragged in all manner of items into the tent. He brought in earth, concrete and unusual looking vegetation. As word spread throughout the campus, more and more people assembled to see what was happening- the third day.

Jeff brought in two big lights, one slightly larger than the other. Bigger crowds gathered all the time. They could hear Jeff work inside the tent and screamed for him to show them what he was doing. Jeff was silent and simply continued to work- the fourth day.

News of the project reached the townspeople and they joined with the students to watch and wonder around the tent. The ever-increasing crowds saw Jeff bring animals, fish and birds of all colors and sizes into the tent- the fifth day.

By the next day the throng of people around the tent stretched for as far as the eye could see. They heard Jeff working, the animals squawking and coupled with the noise from the gathered crowd, it was almost deafening. The mayor called out to Jeff, who poked his head outside the tent wall. Jeff said if they left him alone for the remainder of this day, the work would be complete- the sixth day.

The sun poked its rays over the horizon. It was the seventh day and the sounds within the tent suddenly stopped. The stunned crowd followed suit. Peace enveloped the entire campus, and it was good.

The next day, Jeff slowly moved outside the tent. He reverently walked over to a rope and pulled. The tent seemed to vanish. What the people saw was almost indescribable. A structure with no real defined shape composed of all manner of materials- metal, concrete, wood, and cloth. It used every color in the rainbow and positively teemed with animals and plants. The people saw it and to them the whole thing seemed like a...monstrosity.

The students hated it. The townspeople hated it. Anyone who saw this creation found no redeeming character about it. The creation was built in a way that no-one even knew how to use it. It had no real walls and there was no way to enter. If there was a purpose to any of its structures, nobody knew what it was. In disappointment, the crowd filtered away from Jeff's creation.

Jeff melted back into the countryside. It was as if he did not exist. For a time the structure simply sat and no-one bothered with it. Then, gradually, professors began to meet around it to simply discuss their work. More time passed and students joined in on the discussions. Out of those discussions new theories developed and were taken to other universities around the world for review and expansion. Leaders and major thinkers in their fields were drawn to the college, and to this structure, to talk of new proposals. Townspeople and visitors joined the millings around the structure.

Jeff dropped by every now and then. He saw people of all types and description talking and working by his creation. The structure itself was not used. Nor did Jeff join in. Yet the structure, his creation, attracted and encouraged others. It was a creation that allowed creation. And Jeff saw all that he made and behold IT WAS VERY GOOD.

Midrash Noach
A Rainbow Connection

Frank Noach was a college student in southern Florida. He was not only a very good student but was hopeful of making the next Olympics as the best archer in the state. His bow was something extra special and to make it his own he painted it in striped glossy colors, just like a rainbow.

The school year was about to end and Frank needed a job for the summer. He found one with a small remote zoo located just off the Everglades. It was an easy job. He fed the animals and cleaned out the various enclosures in the morning. He would meander in the afternoon, helping when needed and working with the few visitors the tiny zoo attracted.

Frank needed a place to practice his archery. He did not wish to practice in the woods, as it wasn't the safest place to go alone, and there was no place within the zoo that would not be in the way of the visitors. When he noticed plenty of unused timber around the zoo, he got an idea. Frank did not have much do to in the afternoon, so he asked the zoo director if he could build a structure on the zoo grounds. Frank could use it for archery practice but it could also be used for zoo gatherings, such as speakers or group meetings. As he could do the construction in the afternoon, it would not interfere with his duties and would not cause extra expense to the zoo. The director agreed.

The structure Frank built was unusual in that it was just one very long room. It was perfect for archery, but also useful as a picnic space or meeting hall for the zoo. Most of the planks available were cast-offs from past zoo jobs. The lumber was rarely straight. The bends and curves of the pieces that formed the sides of the building made it look like the hull of a boat. The zoo director liked it. The building was functional, blended with the surroundings and had character; Frank liked it because it was a perfect indoor practice arena.

Frank was going about his morning duties when the wind suddenly began to blow fierce enough that it was difficult to stand. The director worked his way over to him and said that a hurricane had formed off the coast. It was heading their way. The weather service told the director to evacuate the area as quickly as possible.

The director said that the workers would have to try to get the visitors moved to a safer location inland. Frank asked what would happen to the zoo animals. The director said that they did not have enough staff to handle the visitors and also move the animals. The people would have to come first. Frank said that he would stay behind to see what he could do. The director said he did not have time to argue with him. If he wanted to stay, he could do so at his own risk.

Not long after everyone left it began to rain. The zoo did not have many animals, but enough that it would be no small task bringing them all to safety. Frank needed to find a shelter big enough for all of them. The only suitable building was the one he built. However, it was dangerous to place all the animals in one room. He needed to divide it in some way. There was not enough wood left to make separate rooms and even if there was, there was not enough time for the construction. Frank spotted some spools of wire the zoo used for fencing leaning against a building, and it gave him an idea.

Frank grabbed his bow and slung his quiver of arrows over his shoulder. He worked his way to the animal enclosures. He first went to the reindeer pen. He used the end of his bow like a shepherd's stick and moved the animals through the wind and rain to the large wood building. He herded them into one area. When they got into the structure, he took out some arrows and shot them into the wall and posts. He quickly took some of the spooled wire and wrapped it from one arrow to the next creating a fence. It took but minutes to secure the reindeer.

He moved from one animal pen to the next and repeated the procedure. The one set of animals he feared most were the snakes. It sent shivers down his back just to see them. Frank took a few arrows and shot them into the wall. He set a plank onto the arrows and tied it off with the wire, creating a shelf. He did the same things on the sides that created a type of box. Frank walked to the snake pen, and used the end of the bow to lift them out. He walked to the building with the snakes coiled around the end of the bow and placed them into the boxed enclosures.

Time was getting short. The wind and rain had picked up their pace. Frank still had to move the birds. For them he simply shot arrows into the side walls, to act as a perch. He got them to stand on his bow while they went from the enclosure to the shelter. He did not understand why they cooperated as they did, flying onto the bow. Perhaps they understood the danger coming.

Frank had no choice but to herd the last of the large animals into the building. There was no more wire, so he could not pen them off. With the end of his bow, he herded the last of the animals into the building, closed the doors and secured them with the last of his arrows.

Rain began to pelt the shelter. The noise was deafening. The torrents of wind and rain shook the building, the wood creaking and groaning at every beat. The animals strangely enough remained calm. They stirred and emitted muffled sounds, but they did not startle and they did not fight.

The rain and wind seemed to last for forty hours. At times Frank worried that the wind might blow the top off the shelter. Small gaps could be seen between the boards, letting in small ripples of water. Lightning flashed, temporarily illuminating the room. The loud crack which always followed made the animals and Frank jump every time. But the building held.

Suddenly, the rained ceased. Frank removed an arrow securing one of the doors. He opened it cautiously and walked onto the veranda. Water, from the surrounding everglades had risen to the bottom step, surrounding the building. Frank noticed that it was still rising. He watched as one step at a time disappeared below the water. Night fell as the tide rose.

Frank could feel the water as it moved up between the floorboards. The herded animals began to stir. Light from the moon pierced through the cracks in the walls and reflected off the bow. From it, Frank could see the rafters above. He hooked the bow onto two arrows stuck on the sidewall and slung himself up. He sat spread-eagled on the rafter to rest. He was exhausted. At this point all he could do was wait and pray. He closed his eyes and fell asleep.

The stir of the animals below woke Frank up. The sun rise lit the room through the porous walls. Looking below he did not see any water on the floor. The animals, still quiet and reserved, seemed unhurt and unaffected. Frank shimmied down a post to the floor and opened one of the doors. The water had receded. Although the forest surrounding the zoo was in a shambles, his building weathered the hurricane and its aftermath just fine.

Frank stepped onto the front porch and heard the rumble of automobiles and trucks coming down the road. The zoo director and a caravan of rescue workers rolled into the small zoo. Stopping in front of Frank's building, the director peered inside. All he could do was smile and shake his head in disbelief. He barked, "Ok, let's get these critters back to their enclosures." There was no need for a thank you or an expression of a job well done. It was understood by all that without Frank's effort the zoo would no longer exist.

Frank turned and gazed at the horizon. He witnessed a huge rainbow spanning the sky. Turning his view inside the building, he noticed his bow centered on the wall upside down. The sun squeezed through the myriad of cracks in the walls and made it shine. Standing on the porch he could view both the bow and the world beyond it. The bow reflected the rainbow in the sky like a mirror. Frank felt a calm peace fill his body and all was right with the world.

Midrash Lekh Lekha
To Go for Yourself

Ilana had a knack for photography. It was her passion, her focus and recently became her profession. The Los Angeles Times recognized her talents and hired her. She accompanied crews in the field to take pictures of the stories they were covering. It wasn't long before Ilana started to win awards for the pictures she took.

One day her mother came to the newspaper to take Ilana to lunch. As they spoke in her office the editor barged into the room utterly frazzled. He told Ilana to accompany a crew to help cover a breaking story. Ilana turned toward her mother and started apologizing for having to miss their lunch date. Ilana's mother spouted in Hebrew, "Lekh, Lekh! - Go, Go!" The editor with a high crackling voice repeated, "Lekh, Lekh!" Ever since that time when the editor, or for that matter any one at the paper, wanted Ilana to do something they always ended with, "Lekh, Lekh!"

No story was too big or too small for Ilana. The way she saw it, this wasn't just her job, it was her responsibility to help when she could. When a request came from the editor or other reporters for Ilana to join them as the photographer for a specific story, it was never turned down, regardless of the subject or location. It is partly what made her a good photographer, the ability to understand and visualize the needs or wants of others. When the requested Lekh came, Ilana never hesitated.

After so many years of Lekh, Lekh, the constant requests began to take their toll. It was not her way to refuse to help. She just could not say no. Then one day Ilana was asked by the editor to help cover an unfolding story of a riot between rival gangs in a rough part of the city. "Lekh, Lekh!" She and the writing crews took off for the area.

As the crew approached the location of the riot, she noticed smoke piling out of a number of buildings. The police sealed the area and began to move squads in. They didn't see Ilana and the crew slip pass the barricade. The sound of gunfire sliced through the air, adding to the chaos of breaking glass, street fights and shouting. Through the swirl of smoke, rioting, chaos and confusion was seen everywhere. People were being thrown from the rooftops as they fought. The sidewalks were littered with bodies. Blood flowed like water through the streets.

As Ilana looked through the lens, the camera focused on this body part or that body part, bloodied, scarred and disjointed. The smell from the already rotting bodies wafted into her nostrils and made her feel nauseous.

The screaming of the still struggling combatants jolted through Sarah as if it were lightning bolts and she began to shake. The newspaper crew noticed that the camera stopped clicking. It was something that never happened before. They looked over to the photographer and noticed she had turned a pale white. Ilana was not moving a muscle. Quickly they grabbed her and left the area.

Her coworkers drove Ilana home. She went directly into her bedroom and closed the door, not even saying a word to her husband. The editor called a number of times trying to see if she was all right, but never got a response. As day slipped into night, Ilana tried to calm herself. She tried to lock out the world. Her senses had been stripped raw and she needed to find a way to collect herself.

She slept off and on through the night but just could not seem to catch hold of herself. Opening the bedroom door well before dawn Ilana darted out of the house. On her way out of the door, as a reflex action, she grabbed her camera. She jumped in her car and began to drive, without a destination, without a sense of direction.

Ilana rolled through the city streets, past tall grey concrete structures and only stopped when the road ended at a long sandy beach which melded into an expanse of seawater. The sun had barely begun to rise and it filled the ocean with a strange purple color. It was a time when it was not yet light but not like the darkness of the middle of the night. Ilana climbed out of the car and grabbed her camera. She walked down to the water's edge and began taking photos. There were photos of the rippling waves, the undulating sands, and the myriad of strange colors and shapes that filled that time of the morning. The beauty was breathtaking. Ilana began to feel control come back into her body.

Ilana spent the whole day on that beach. She took pictures of different people that happened by. She caught a skateboarder sliding down a steel handrail. She took a picture of a mother and daughter making geometric shapes with their fingers in the sand. She took a picture of a sea bird standing on one leg on a stump in the middle of the water, taking an afternoon siesta.

With each picture she felt stronger and better. It was as if some life force began to trickle into her like an empty well drinking in the rain. Ilana had always taken pictures but this was different. For the first time the pictures she took were for herself- Lekh Lekha!

By the end of the day Ilana felt like her old self. She returned home and kissed her husband and children. The following day she was back at work. She reassured the editor that she was fine. She just needed to get away for a short spell. Ilana did go back to helping others, "Lekh, Lekh!" Yet she now understood that in the framework of her life there needed to be a little me time. In the future Ilana set aside time just for herself. This was not a selfish act but one that helped her cope with the rest of the world. There was a time for Lekh Lekha.

Midrash Vayeira
Hospitality

Abraham met Sarah in college. As if fate had drawn
them together, much like their Biblical namesakes, they fell in
love and married. The couple settled in the Boston area, just
off of downtown. They loved the hustle and bustle of city life.
To them, the parks, the plays, the myriad of people and the
constant commotion was cherished.

One Friday, while walking home from work, Abraham
passed a couple huddled on the side of the road, distraught and
sad. Abraham asked politely if he could help. The man said
he had lost his job and that he and his wife had been traveling
from town to town trying to find work. Their car literally ran
out of gas and they had no more money.

Abraham, without hesitation, brought them to his house and fed them a nice warm Shabbat meal. They spent the whole weekend with Abraham and Sarah. On Monday Abraham made a call to an old friend and was able to find work for his troubled guests. He helped them move into a temporary housing development that allowed them to save enough money over time to get a place of their own. Sarah and Abraham talked often of how this small kind act made them feel so good.

Some time later, a major client of Abraham's came into Boston on business. Abraham remember how this man hated staying in hotels, how he complained that they were always so lonely and impersonal. Abraham volunteered to have him stay at his house. The client remarked the next day how comfortable he felt in Abraham and Sarah's home.

Abraham's hospitality spread. When guests came in to speak at the synagogue, they would always stay at Abraham and Sarah's. Soon even guests of the mayor found their way into their home. No one could quite figure out what made the place so comfortable. They wondered how Abraham and Sarah knew exactly how the put their lodgers at ease. Over the years, guests sent a small thank you in the form of various small presents. Just little knickknacks and decorations, but soon their home was filled with items of interest that were colorful and pleasing to the eye. Each gift was not only nice to look at, but acted as a reminder, a connection, to the wonderful people and personalities of the people that stayed there.

One evening, just passed midnight, Abraham and
Sarah were roused by a crash in the house. They got out of
bed and started toward the front door. Four men had broken
into the house. They wore masks over their heads, and
pointed guns at Abraham and Sarah. They fired a warning
shot through the living room couch, spraying stuffing up into
the air. Sara and Abraham did not make a move. One of the
men took duct tape and covered their mouths; another took
rope and bound them together, setting them on the floor.

The thieves ran through the house throwing anything
they could into large duffle bags. What would not fit was
smashed by the firearms they held. In the blink of an eye the
entire residence was ramshackled. Abraham noticed, through
the dust and darkness, two of the thieves talking at the side.
They picked up small metal canisters and turned them upside
down. Abraham recognized the smell of gas in the air.

Another of the masked men came over, clenched the
rope surrounding Abraham and Sarah and dragged them
across the floor. Shards of broken glass and shattered ceramics
cut and scarred their bodies as they moved toward the door.
Suddenly there was a flash of light and fire engulfed the
residence.

The thieves left Abraham and Sarah on the sidewalk as
they escaped into the night. Fire trucks and police soon arrived
at the scene. The police untied the couple and brought them
to an ambulance while the firemen unsuccessfully fought the
blaze. In less than an hour the house was a pile of smoldering
rubble. The ambulance took Sarah and Abraham to the
hospital. Doctors treated the wounds, patched them up and
placed them in a room to try to get some sleep.

The next morning, before checking into a hotel, Sarah and Abraham went to a café directly across from their house. They sat sipping coffee by the window, looking across the street, lamenting over the ashen pile, smoke still slowly meandering up into the air. They were sad, confused, perplexed. What had they done to cause such a catastrophe? Is the world filled with so much evil that even their small abode was not shielded? It was not just the material loss, but the sense of feeling personally violated that racked the very essence of their souls.

Sitting at the window Sarah noticed construction machinery moving down the street. Large pieces of equipment stopped in front of their property. Bulldozers crept off of the trailers and scooped up the ash and rubble, depositing it in trucks that continually appeared in front of the site. In a manner of a few hours the fired pile of rubble was gone.

Other trucks, trailers and men arrived. Wood, brick, and all sorts of equipment were unloaded. For some time the former residential site of Abraham and Sarah looked like a beehive. Men and women diligently working in different trades constructed a new home. The news agencies picked up the story. As word spread about what was happening, gifts from all those who spent time in their residence filled the very coffee shop that Abraham and Sarah spent time seeing the new house appear. The new presents were sent to replace the lost artifacts. It was a way for those outside the community, recipients of Abraham and Sarah's hospitality, to contribute to the reconstruction effort.

Abraham and Sarah did not know what to make of
what was going on. They tried to find the source of the activity.
Yet no one origin could be found. What became apparent was
that the entire community felt an attachment, some tie, to
Sarah and Abraham. As much as their house was a physical
source of hospitality for outsiders, it was also a key site of pride
and involvement for the whole community. The city residents
felt it their responsibility to act. They could not change or stop
what the robbers did. But they could lend a hand to rebuild, to
reinvigorate, and to help a couple that had helped so many
unselfishly.

The day Abraham and Sarah moved back into their
house was marked by a citywide celebration. Thousands
gathered at the site. Television cameras with their lights high
up in the air made it seem like a Hollywood opening. It was a
festive occasion marked by speeches and dancing and singing.
Tears flowed down both Abraham and Sarah's cheeks as they
felt the kavanah, the love that engulfed the surrounding area. It
was only now that they realized how the small acts of hospitality
they had extended to others affected so many. That the people
of the city, their guests, as well as themselves, felt part of those
acts, and it was something that brought the whole community
together.

Midrash Chayei Sarah
A Cup of Water

Isaac was president of one of the largest book suppliers in the city. He specialized in textbooks for schools. Each year there was an annual summer buyer's convention where suppliers would gather to show their new lines. Normally Isaac would go, but this year, due to his advancing age and the fact that he was not feeling so well, he decided to send one of his trusted employees, Elijah. Elijah himself was no youngster, but he did not mind the travel.

The convention was to open on Sunday morning. Elijah decided to leave Friday afternoon, so as not to have to travel on Shabbat. As the convention was not too far away, he decided to drive and take his pet dog along. The dog was small and unobtrusive. He made a good traveling companion and Elijah did not want to place him in a kennel for the weekend.

Elijah checked into a hotel and felt he had time to take the dog for a walk and explore the surrounding area. It was extremely hot for this time of year but after the ride he thought that they both needed to get out and stretch their muscles. Within a few blocks they both started panting from the stifling air.

They stopped and rested on some steps of an apartment building. A young woman exited the structure and approached. She noticed through a window how uncomfortable they seemed and brought a large glass of ice water to him and a bowl of water for the dog.

Elijah inquired as to her name. It was Rebecca. He thanked her very much for the water. He asked if she knew of a local synagogue, as he made it a habit to always attend a service on Friday evening. She said that there were a number to choose from, but if he would like, he could join her family at their synagogue. She said the service they attended was most unusual and thought he would enjoy it. Rebecca invited Elijah to join them for a Shabbat meal and afterward he could walk to the synagogue with her family. His dog could remain in the apartment after dinner where there was air conditioning.

At dinner he met Rebecca's father, mother and brother. The brother sat at the head of the table. He led a prayer over the wine and bread before the meal was served. The father sat at his side. He had a blank stare and barely moved. The brother noticed Elijah staring at the father. He said that his father had a stroke some months ago and never did recover. He could not speak or work.

As the food was placed on the table Elijah asked what kind of work the brother did. He responded that he ran a supply store for sheep farmers. He had customers from all over the country. Elijah took a closer look around the room. There were some very nice furnishings. Even the tablecloth for the Shabbat meal was made of fine lace. The brother must have made a very nice living.

The conversation throughout dinner was pleasant but superficial. Then the brother asked Elijah what city he came from. With Elijah's answer the room suddenly became eerily quiet. A few moments later the brother spouted, "Rebecca, isn't that the locale of the university you thought you might go to?" Rebecca responded, "Unless forced to be a bird in a gilded cage, it *is* the locale of the university I will be going to this next fall!" The brother explained to Elijah that no female in their family ever left the city before. They had all gone to school here, so they could live at home. The remainder of the meal was covered with a tense, stifling aura, as the brother and Rebecca shot silent glances toward each other.

Shortly after the meal the family walked to the synagogue which was located but a few blocks away. As they approached a building Elijah noticed people standing in a line that stretched around the block. He figured it must have been for a rock concert or some other venue. It turned out that this was the synagogue. He never saw anything like it before, people lined up prior to a Friday night service, just to attend a synagogue! Rebecca told him that people began to line up hours before the start and that this was typical every Friday night.

They entered the building. It must have held over two thousand people. Every age could be seen, young, old and even babies cradled by their mothers. The synagogue had a balcony and even that was full! People continued to file into the already crowded building. They stood in the aisle ways and along the back walls. Elijah had never seen such a sight. Normally only a few hundred attended his synagogue on a Friday night.

Elijah soon found out why. The service was done in song from start to finish. And the songs were not solemn low-keyed reverent tunes but upbeat, loud, harmonious and joyous. Rebecca explained that the tradition of being solemn at a Shabbat service was only a recent invention. It was thought by the rabbis that services to welcome Shabbat in biblical days were done with exuberant singing and musical instruments. This congregation wanted to enjoy, celebrate and welcome Shabbat in this manner.

The singing was beautiful. The congregation harmonized together. During a rendition of Lecha Dodi, a song welcoming Shabbat, people even got up to dance. As he looked around Elijah noticed people smiling, holding hands, and talking with each other. It gave a real sense of community.

After services a curtain was pulled back and tables of cakes, sweets and drinks were revealed. It was a tradition at this synagogue to have an oneg, by definition meaning joy, but usually associated with the congregation sharing food together. Rebecca, Elijah and the brother sauntered over to the tables. Rebecca reached for a slice of beautiful cake, layered in white fluffy frosting with the decoration of a tree imprinted in the top. As she moved a piece of it toward her mouth, Elijah knocked it out of her hand onto the floor. "Why would you do such a thing?" Rebecca spouted. The brother grabbed Elijah's lapel and was beginning to raise his fist. Elijah responded, "Don't you smell it?" "Smell what", retorted the brother. "Almonds, rotten almonds!" Elijah said. "And what of it?" the brother said. "It is not an Almond Cake! There is something not right with this food", said Elijah.

One of the congregants noticed a note tucking out from under the cake. He slid it out, opened it and read it aloud. "There is no place on this earth for Jews. Jews are God's leftovers and nothing more. I'm disgusted by your race and your ways. You don't belong on this planet; you should be exterminated from the face of earth." The stunned, silent congregants quickly exited the building, amidst the sounds of police alarms approaching. The brother released Elijah and apologized.

A police investigator took a bit of the cake and placed a few drops of a solution on it. It turned dark blue. The investigator announced the cake had been laced with cyanide. "I didn't smell anything, how did you?" asked the brother. "Not everyone is sensitive to the smell but I am." responded Elijah.

After being interrogated by the police, the three began to walk back to the apartment. The brother began to lament, "How can such hatred, such venom exist in this world. How can God allow such people to exist?" Elijah and Rebecca remained silent. The brother continued after a few more minutes of silence. "I want to thank you for saving my sister. You were very kind to intervene." Elijah responded, "Rebecca began this kindness with the offer of water to a stranger and his pet... but we must remember that water is not always welcome!" With that Elijah lifted the brother off the edge of the sidewalk and placed him on the grass well away from the street, as a street washing machine came by spraying water onto the area the brother recently inhabited. "Perhaps it is the kindness between people we should try to remember." Elijah resounded.

The brother agreed to let Rebecca attend the university as Elijah said his family would be honored to look after any needs she may have while in their city. Elijah told Rebecca that when she arrived to please call and they would help her move in. He would also like to return the favor and have her spend a Shabbat with them. He told her that the head of the company had a son that was her age and was also starting at the local university.

Elijah wanted to give something to Rebecca for all the kindness she had shown him. He reached into his pocket and pulled out two beautiful bracelets. "I saw these the other day and purchased them because I liked the imprint on them. But after the cake incident, I thought you should have them." He handed the bracelets to Rebecca. Embossed on the metal were beautiful trees, the same design as was on the cake. She said she could not accept such a gift. Elijah asked her to keep them and when she came to town and if she still felt that way she could return the bracelets. She agreed.

28

A few months later Rebecca arrived. Elijah picked her up at the airport. Rebecca was wearing the two bracelets. They were to go by Isaac's house to pick up his son and move them both to the university. The son was outside as the car approached the house. When Rebecca exited the car, Isaac's son met her, offering a cup of water.

Midrash Toldot
An Heirloom

Harold and Jacob were twins. Although born at the same time, they were as different as one could possibly imagine. Harold was rugged, broad, athletic and headstrong as they come. When he was born he was covered with hair. Jacob was small in stature, was born bald, liked books and did not especially like to participate in outdoor games. He was a cerebral kind of person who always thought before making a decision.

The family was typical. The twin's father worked as an architect for a small firm, their mother did a little interior decorating as she kept an eye on the boys. There were no other brothers or sisters. Their mother had a hard time getting pregnant and it was a real surprise to learn that at a reasonably advanced age she was to have twins.

The family lived in a nice house, in a nice neighborhood. There was nothing special about their house, with one exception. The family had an heirloom. It was a Torah scroll that had been handed down through so many generations that no one really knew how it was originally received. Their father built a cabinet with a glass front door to display the scroll in the living room. A thick red velvet cover protected the parchment scroll. The cover contained a small imprint Chai, the Hebrew word for life, at the very bottom. Jacob noticed that the velvet was stained different colors in a number of areas and had asked his mother about it. She said that when he and his brother were a little older she would explain. It became a tradition that on each birthday, the boys would go to their mother to see if she would now tell them about the Torah cover, but their mother always said, "When you are a little older".

The Torah heirloom did have a special place in their lives. Whenever a member of the immediate or extended family would have a Bar or Bat Mitzvah, it was this scroll that they read from at the synagogue. They also used it for holidays like Simchat Torah when they would parade their scroll, alongside others at the synagogue. On other occasions it was taken out on Shabbat and read from as well.

When the boys were small they would often play together. As the boys grew older they grew more distant from each other. By the time they were teenagers they made separate friends and spent little time together. As young men they both married and moved to separate parts of the country to ply their jobs. They would meet at special family get-togethers, and were cordial to each other but seemed to have little in common.

A baby boy was born to Jacob and his wife. They were to have a Brit Milah (the Jewish circumcision ritual done when a baby boy is eight days old) at their parent's house. The whole family was invited. Harold, after much prodding, agreed to attend and spend the weekend. The ceremony was beautiful. They set an empty chair next to the torah cabinet for Elijah and set the Torah scroll on that seat after taking it out of the case for the ceremony. After the commotion of the celebratory day, the twins, their wives and their parents sat and conversed the night away, eventually dispersing to various parts of the house to sleep.

Late that night alarms began to go off. Jacob woke to see an onrush of water into the house from the outside. Looking through a window he noticed power lines laying in the road and houses across the way on fire. Water gushed from broken water mains on the street flooding everything on the block.

Jacob's wife ran to their newborn. Earlier in the evening he had been set on a small portable mattress on the floor to sleep. On entering the baby's room she noticed the water had floated the mattress to one of the corners. Rushing to the baby she noticed he was bleeding. The mattress had been deflated by a sharp vent handle that then sliced into the baby's stomach. Jacob's wife screamed seeing the blood seep into the surrounding water. The screech brought Jacob flying into the room. He picked up his crying son and began moving toward the front door. He pressed his hands against the baby's stomach to try to stop the bleeding. It did not do the job. The other family members were exiting the house as fast as they could. Jacob had to find a way to stop the bleeding. He needed a tourniquet.

Passing through the living room Jacob spotted the Torah. Without a second thought he broke the glass front and grabbed the velvet cover off the scroll. Jacob tied the cloth in a knot around the baby so as to place pressure against the wound. At first blood oozed from beneath the velvet but then, miraculously, it stopped. Harold running up behind, saw what was happening and grabbed the now naked Torah parchment. Both headed out of the house.

Jacob was able to get the baby to a hospital and they treated the wound. A small scar remained but other than that he was fine. Jacob asked for the velvet cover back and a hospital worker complied.

A few days later the families met at a cousin's house. Jacob tried to get the bloodstains off the velvet cover but even the commercial cleaners could not remove the new stains. Jacob tried to apologize to his parents but they did not seem to listen. They took the velvet cover and placed it over the scroll.

The mother turned to the boys and said it was time to explain about the Torah. First, it could only go to one of the boys. Although their father had always hoped they could share the responsibility, it had been a tradition that only one could be responsible for the heirloom. It had been that way throughout the generations and it would remain so now. The boys looked at each other. They both knew that Harold had saved the scroll from the water, coupled with being the first born, the heirloom most certainly would go to him.

The mother went on. "We do not have a record as to who first possessed this family heirloom. Yet, for different generations, the cover had served many strange purposes. One of our ancestors was exiled from Spain and had used the scroll and cover as a type of baby carrier as they traveled to their new

home. The incident had left a stain on the cover. Another
ancestor's baby got very sick. The doctors had instructed the
parents to keep the baby as warm as possible. They took the
velvet cover, wrapped the baby in it and placed it as close to the
fire as possible. The baby survived but the incident left a stain
on the cover. Another ancestor was attacked while forced from
his home. A sword was thrust through the cover just missing
the scroll. However it pierced the carrier in the arm.
Bloodied, our ancestor made his way to safety, still carrying the
Torah. The incident left a stain on the cover"

Their mother told story after story. It seemed to last
for hours. The common thread to all the stories was that this
Torah, and most especially the cover, was linked with the
sanctity of life. The stains on the cover were not removed
because they were a badge, a reminder, that life was always
more important than the words themselves. The words,
although an important symbol, had to be translated into action.
And it was the action that held the meaning. It was to be Jacob
who would be responsible for the heirloom.

Midrash Vayeitzei
The Ladder

Joshua belonged to a family that just did not make much sense to him. There was his father, mother and brother, but any semblance of a relationship was purely accidental. They never ate meals together, never went on trips together and barely even saw each other through the week.

Joshua had begun building a project for school on a basement table and had it just about finished, when a friend called to invite him to play baseball at the fields. When Joshua returned, he found the project moved, and in so doing, badly damaged his work. His brother was watching television when Joshua approached him asking if he moved the project. His brother said yes, he moved it, and said "now get out of here and leave me alone". Joshua went berserk. He rushed at his brother, jumping on his back, flaying away with his arms.

Joshua's brother was older and stronger. At first he was caught by surprise and Joshua got in a few good licks, but he had quickly recovered and now had Joshua on the floor giving him far more than he bargained for. Joshua, trying to escape, was able to get his leg in a position to flip his brother. After doing so, he realized he would get hurt if he stayed and fought, so ran from the house and skirted down the block.

Joshua was angry and hurt. He could not go back to the house so decided to walk where ever his feet would carry him, and as far away from his family as possible. He walked for hours and was getting tired. He found an old warehouse building and stumbled on an unlocked door. The inside of the warehouse was huge. There were no interior walls and the roof seemed to stretch forever. Joshua snuggled into a dark corner and fell asleep.

When Joshua opened his eyes he could hardly believe what he saw. In fact he could not tell if what he saw was real or if this was a dream. A circus had moved into the building, set up their equipment and were practicing their acts. There were people and animals and equipment everywhere he looked.

As Joshua stumbled around, the circus folk simply ignored him. Joshua turned to view another part of the building and became awestruck. In the very center of the warehouse there was a huge ladder.

This was not just any ladder and certainly not a kind that he had ever seen before. The ladder had fluorescent colored rungs and not one rung seemed the same color as another. The two side rails were also different colors and twisted as it moved up in the air. It was as if the ladder was a helix that stretched from the ground up so high that the top could not be seen. To complete the visual amazement, a whole troop of people moved up and down the ladder. Yet Joshua could find no wires or ropes that steadied or fixed the ladder in place.

Joshua approached one of the men just exiting the bottom part of the ladder. He asked him what was going on. The man said that it was a circus and they were practicing for the shows they were to give in the next few days. Joshua asked how the ladder remained steady and in place. The man said it was the teamwork of his family.

Joshua gasped! "You mean to tell me that all these men are your relatives?" The man smiled and said, "Yep all twelve of us are brothers and you probably can just make out my sister toward the top. In fact you can help us out a little bit. We know each other so well that practice becomes too routine. We often ask strangers to climb with us so we can practice our adjustments, working together, to make sure the ladder does not fall. It makes practice far more interesting. Would you be interested in climbing the ladder?"

Without thinking much about his slight fear of heights, Joshua agreed and began climbing the ladder. The man said that Joshua needed to help the others by feeling how the ladder moved in unison with the other climbers. As he went up rung by rung, Joshua began to feel the slight ebbs and flows of the other climbers through the ladder. The more he climbed, the more he felt.

Joshua could see the brothers as they moved down the other side or climbing above and below him. It was like a ballet. As Joshua reached the top, the helical twist of the ladder allowed a smooth transition to the downward portion of the trip. A few minutes later Joshua was firmly back on the ground. The ladder had not moved from its original position.

Joshua felt something inside his body and it was a feeling he never had before. He asked one of the brothers if he ever felt something inside when he climbed the ladder. The brother smiled and said, "You always feel that way when you climb"! Joshua asked, "What is that feeling?" Another of the brothers interrupted and said it is when you work so well with others that you feel their heartbeat along with your own. It gives one a sense of community, a sense of belonging and a sense of the beat of life itself.

One of the brothers invited Joshua to have a meal with them. The parents, brothers, and sister, all sat at the same large circular table. A small prayer was said at the beginning of the meal, in a low respectful tone by the father, followed by plenty of food, plenty of conversation and plenty of good natured kidding. The feeling when climbing the ladder was present even when sitting around the table. It was not just some momentary connection but one that pervaded the family and all those who, even for a few small moments, touched their lives.

Joshua left the circus and walked for miles. He shook his head in disbelief. It was as if he was coming out of a dream. He did not know if what he saw was real or not. Joshua wanted to go home.

On his return, he decided that something had to change with his own family. He wanted more of what he had felt with the circus family. He went to the kitchen and made a large wonderful meal. He called his father at work and his mother at her friend's house and asked if they would please come home. He knocked on his brother's door and asked that they stop fighting, if for just the evening, and invited him to join the family for dinner.

The father, mother and brother were amazed that Joshua put forth such effort with this meal. Joshua asked his father to say a small prayer before he served the food. His father winced but complied. The family enjoyed the meal, had a little conversation and was at least cordial to each other. It was a start.

The mailman brought a small package to the house that was addressed to Joshua. He opened the package and a small note dropped out. It was from the circus troupe. It said that Joshua dropped his school ID when climbing the ladder. They had enjoyed their time together, and since his address was on the ID, they wanted to mail it back with a small token of thanks for helping them out on that day. On pushing the wrapping paper back, Joshua exposed a tiny multicolored ladder, twisted like the one at the circus. He smiled. It was not just a dream.

Over the next few weeks Joshua's family saw each other more often, and were far more cordial than he could ever remember. It still was not the warmest place on earth but at least it moved in a positive direction. Joshua vowed that when he was a father, his family would be one that would spend time together and enjoy one another. He wanted the feel of the ladder to be with his family always.

Midrash Vayishlach
The Meaning of a Name

Mark was the best wrestler in the state. He may have been the best wrestler in the country. He was big, muscular and had an instinct for exactly how to finish an opponent quickly and efficiently. He started wrestling when he was very young, and as he grew it became part of his being. Mark was very popular. As he wrestled throughout his school career, people would come from far and wide to see him ply his sport.

During one of his tournaments, he learned a move that the crowds loved. Using leverage, he picked up his opponent and slammed him down in a way to cause the mat to emit a sound that can best be described as "crishhh". The people in the stands stood and screamed in unison, "crishhh, crishhh, crishhh"- until Mark stood up and waved. They roared their approval and continued to call out, "crishhh, crishhh, crishhh". This special ovation followed him from tournament to tournament.

While on the wrestling team in college, the government asked for the school to send the team on a goodwill tour to Mexico. It was part of a cultural exchange between governments. The team packed up and traveled on a whirlwind tour in which they wrestled volunteer residents in eighteen different cities. The newspapers had publicized the tour so well that by the time the team left, a group of over one hundred and twenty accompanied them, at their own expense. As Mark wrestled time and again, the crowd, in their now famous cheer, would scream loudly, "crishhh, crishhh, crishhh", every time Mark would both begin and end one of his always successful bouts.

The tour seemed to take the wind out of Mark. After only six days of constant exhibitions and travel, everything was a blur. On that evening he tossed and turned and just could not relax enough to sleep. Finally, as the first rays poked over the horizon, he decided to go jogging to try to get his mind and body back in sync.

As he moved through street after winding street, his mind melded with the rhythm of his feet. Mark rounded one of the blocks and heard a scream for help coming from one of the shack dwellings. What was unusual was that the language was English and he could not remember hearing anything but Spanish being spoken throughout their tour.

He poked his head into the shack where a doctor was bent over a small boy, his hands positioned through an incision in the boy's body. The doctor was Mexican but had developed an unusual habit when stressed to speak English, in which he was fluent. Mark asked if he could help. He said that the boy had an inflamed appendix and that it had to come out. If it was not removed, it would burst in the boy's body and he would die. The problem was that if he moved his hands from the sides of the incision, it would cause the inflamed appendix to burst. The doctor had to hold open the incision while another set of hands would have to lift the organ up so he could make the cut, and then, the organ would have to be moved outside the body before it broke open.

Without hesitation Mark placed his hands inside the incision, cradled the appendix and slowly lifted. The doctor cut the two ends and tied them off. Mark in a slow smooth careful motion lifted the bulging appendix out of the boy and placed it in a bucket at the side of the cot. As soon as it hit the bottom of the bucket, it burst and disintegrated. The doctor finished closing the incision and thanked Mark. He said that if he had not come along at that time the boy most certainly would have died.

The parents of the boy went up to Mark, clasped his hands into theirs and said in a low thankful voice, "crishhh, crishhh, crishhh". Mark was stunned. These people could not possibly have known of his wrestling. The doctor said that in their particular dialect crishhh meant "one who gives life through kindness". It was the highest compliment that could be given in this village.

Mark made his way back to where the team was staying. He said nothing of the amazing experience he had that day. The next time he took to the wrestling mat, the crowd in their usual fashion cheered their famous cry both before and after the inevitable victory. Yet for Mark, that cheer, now and forever, held a far different meaning.

Midrash Vayeishev
A Coat of Many Colors

Josephine was the best clothing designer in the United States. And she knew it. What set her aside from all of her competition was the use of color in her work. It was not just color but the use of many colors all at the same time. It made the clothes, and any person who wore them, stand out, even in a crowd. The current trend for other designers was the use of black and different shades of gray.

Show after designer show, Josephine was a major success. Her competitors also benefited from her line, as many buyers attended these shows and purchased their products as well, just not in the same quantity. Josephine let the competition know it too. She lauded her success over them as she pranced through the audience during the shows, not only promoting her own line, but also putting her competitors down. The competitors were not only jealous of Josephine but grew to hate her.

The designers had enough of this lady and decided to do something about it. The largest show of the year was about to begin. Just prior to the show, the other clothing company representatives stood just outside the building, answering questions and milling around with the public. They huddled together at the side when they saw Josephine's limousine approaching from blocks away, already visible from its loud multi-color design. When Josephine exited the car, flashing a dress and coat that would make your eyes squint, one of the other designers met her and moved her to the side where her compatriots were waiting. The group formed a tight circle and slowly enveloped Josephine as they moved her toward the center. She disappeared into the circle of black that the other designers wore.

When Josephine hit the center, someone pushed a button on the side of the building, opening a trap door, normally used to bring food into the building. Josephine dropped into a dark, dank pit. Just before her fall, one of the other designers stripped the multi-color coat off Josephine. At the bottom of the pit, a group of hired men sprayed dark muddy water over the coat, covering the loud colors, making its appearance drab and nondescript. They bound and carted Josephine away.

As the show started, Josephine was nowhere to be found. It proceeded without her as the building crew searched for Josephine. They found only her coat, drenched in mud. The show itself was a disaster. Without Josephine and her colors, the buyers seemed to lose interest. They bought nothing from any of the designers. The coat was given to the police who felt she was probably abducted and most likely killed.

The other designers had arranged for Josephine to be kidnapped but not killed. They did not want that on their conscience. They had her flown out of the country, taken to a small town in France and dropped on the side of the road. While in transit the kidnappers ripped the rest of her clothes off and dressed her in the drabbest filthy clothes they could find.

Josephine sat stunned. At first it was quite beyond her comprehension why anyone would do this to her. The shock of being kidnapped placed Josephine in a daze. She slowly wandered around the French town pondering, wondering what caused others to act this way toward her. A local family, who felt sorry for such a sad sight, befriended Josephine. They brought her in, fed her and cleaned up her tattered clothes. Josephine was humble and thankful for the help.

Over the next week she began to interact with this family and other local townspeople. The communication was at first tentative but over time grew friendly, warm and comfortable. There was nothing rough or loud about the relationships, only a bond that grew with each interaction. It then dawned on Josephine. Her behavior toward others must have been the cause of her rejection. In her professional life she knew she was loud and brash. She thought it a show, but others apparently took it personally.

While having coffee one day with her adopted family, their little girl ran up quite sad and forlorn. She was chosen to be in a school play but needed a costume, one that required many bright colors. The mother did not know what to do.

Josephine spoke up and said that she could take care of the problem. She and the little girl went through the village collecting different colored cloths and brought them back to the house where Josephine wove together a perfect dress for the occasion.

The play for the little girl was a success and it happened that some designers from Paris were visiting the village and saw the show. They inquired about the dress and were introduced to Josephine. They immediately connected and Josephine was offered work in Paris. She moved and became very successful, a second time, in her line of work.

The designer business in the United States was dreadful. The companies decided they needed to expand into the European market to try to revive their business. They decided to attend a French fashion show the following week. As the show began multi-colored dresses emerged from the wings. No word needed to be spoken by the designers. The mark of Josephine was in plain view.

Josephine noticed her former competitors in the audience. She had a stage hand invite them back stage to meet. The designers were not sure what to do but decided to go through with the meeting. As the designers moved backstage, they noticed a number of policemen encircling the group. Josephine could be seen standing on a platform above and to the side, arms folded, and a stern expression frozen on her face. The police slowly moved in tightening the sphere. The designers were frightened and did not quite know what to expect.

Suddenly confetti rained down upon the designers. The police broke out in laughter and dispersed. Josephine moved to the designers smiling. She hugged and kissed each one of them. Stunned, the designers remained motionless.

Josephine reassured the designers that nothing would happen to them. She explained that she knew what they did and why. Although she was not pleased with what they did to her, she understood. The event opened her eyes and changed her life.

She said that she was quite happy in France and would make her home there. She offered a line of her clothes to be marketed by them in the States. They would form a partnership and both would benefit from the exchange. Thrilled and bewildered, the designers agreed.

Josephine would live her days out in France. Her designs, widely accepted and successful, made her wealthy and admired. Yet Josephine found her greatest enjoyment spending weekends back in that little village. She not only maintained a home there but set up designer classes for the villagers and took an active role in the community. She still loved using many colors within the same design. The loudness however was confined to the clothes; her life and demeanor was peaceful, tranquil and fulfilling.

Midrash Mikeitz
The Dream

Jon was the head of the Agricultural Department and member of the President's Cabinet. He had put in an exhausting week and dragged himself into his apartment, dropping his ever-bulging briefcase on the floor and headed straight for the bedroom. As he approached the bed he began to unloosen his tie. The effort was almost too much and he fell head first across the bed, falling right asleep.

His phone rang annoyingly and woke him up. It was not just any phone but a special one placed in his apartment with a line straight from the White House. He remembered thinking it a joke that they made the phone red and it lit up when it rang. Jon answered. He needed to come directly to the White House. There was a crisis that required a full Cabinet meeting. Jon dragged himself out of bed, still not quite awake, brushed himself off and headed for the car.

48

Prior to the meeting, his staff briefed him. They had collected data for months and their conclusions were undeniable. They handed him the pages of proofs and sent him off to the meeting.

The meeting began very upbeat. The other cabinet members were excited and happy. When the meeting started each cabinet member in turn expressed his or her joy over the worldwide abundance of grain. It seemed that the weather conditions made it perfect for growth not only in the United States but everywhere around the world.

Then it was Jon's turn. His face was not happy. He did not quite know how to break the news. It turned out that the data collected by his department did indicate a global condition that allowed for the major growth. Based on the data his department collected, this anomaly would last for seven years. The problem was that the data also indicated that for seven years thereafter the conditions would reverse to the point that almost no grain would be able to be grown.

The room grew quiet. Then laughter broke out. The other members thought Jon was playing a joke. But his facial expression did not change and after a few minutes the laughter died down to a ghostly silence. The president asked what could be done, assuming they believed his data. Jon said that if he were the president he would divert money from the budget, build as many storage silos as possible and fill them with grain over the next seven years.

The room exploded with fury. If they diverted funds then the other cabinet programs would be diminished or stopped. This did not please the other cabinet members, as it would adversely affect their constituents. They said that in the history of the world, although famine has always been present in parts of the globe, it never covered the whole earth and certainly never lasted for seven years.

The president had to make a decision. If Jon were right it would affect billions of people. The president was confused, bewildered. The popular move would have been to listen to the majority of cabinet members. He reasoned that their voices outweighed Jon's data. Finally he made a resolve. He would not divert funds. He felt that even if Jon were right, the scientists around the world would figure a way out of the problem. He also knew that seven years from now he would not be president so it would not be his problem to solve.

The president went on television to talk to the nation and the world about the great abundance of grain. People cheered all around the globe. Leaders congratulated themselves on what a wonderful job they were doing, taking credit for the great harvest.

For Jon the next seven years went like the flash of a light bulb. He was asked by the new administration to stay on as Head of Agriculture. Jon agreed but worried as the seven years of plenty headed toward an end.

At the beginning of the eighth year the weather dramatically changed. Reports started to come in as famine spread. Countries begged other countries to export food that they did not have. Even in the United States, no grain could be found. The pictures on the television grew more and more gruesome as time went on. Battles fought, wars waged, people died. And the famine stretched on.

Jon, and his staff, spent untold hours looking for a solution, any solution, or even something that could forestall the effects of the famine. If only the president had listened. Hour after exhausting hour they worked. Jon, his nerves frayed beyond repair, needed rest. He drove home and stumbled into his apartment, dropping his ever-bulging briefcase on the floor and headed straight for the bedroom. As he approached the bed he began to unloosen his tie. The effort was almost too much and he fell head first across the bed, falling right asleep.

His phone rang annoyingly and woke him up...

Midrash Vayigash
The Disguise

Simon loved to be a father. It was his reason for being. He and his wife had a little girl. He cherished her and spent as much time as he could while she was growing up. When she was only two they started a routine. On his way home from work on Friday he would stop by a book store and purchase something they would read that night, together, just before she went to sleep.

Although they would always read what Simon brought home that day, they always ended each Friday evening with a short favorite. It was called "Dreamland". The front of the book had different pictures on it, each within a cloud formation. There were cows in one of the clouds, stalks of grain in another and people in others. The stories inside were not too good but the two of them just seemed to love them.

52

They had read the words so often that they had the
book memorized. After the reading they would hug each other
and say "I love you". He would tuck her in bed, kiss her on
the forehead, turn out the lights and leave the room. His
daughter was now six, and they both still looked forward to
every Friday night.

Simon left his office one bright shiny Friday and
headed for the bookstore. As he entered the clerks gave him a
familiar smile and waved hello. He headed for the aisles where
the children's books were displayed. Just as he reached them
the glass front of the store shattered. Simon heard the rattling
of gunfire from all directions. He felt something pierce his
shoulder blade and warm blood began to ooze out of the
puncture wound. He fell to the floor.

Simon landed on his side. Half his body was back
behind the book stacks but his head landed in the aisle way.
Blood, still flowing from the wound, soon pooled around his
body. He noticed a number of men enter the store, all with
guns. Then an older large man slowly opened one of the
shattered glass doors and came in. He walked toward another
man huddled in the corner. He introduced himself to the
cornered man and said that he would no longer stand by and
watch him try to take over his territory. He pulled out a gun
and shot the man point blank in his temple.

The boss motioned to the other gun toting men and
told them to make sure everyone else in the store was dead.
He did not want anyone talking to the police. The men spread
out and began to check the bodies lying on the floor. They
approached Simon. The henchman tried to avoid the puddled
blood and one of them kicked Simon. He did not flinch. The
men thought him dead and moved toward other bodies. Those
that did move were greeted with a few more rounds of bullets.

The boss and his men left the building. Simon remembered hearing sirens and the flash of a few policemen as they entered the store before he passed out from the loss of blood. Simon woke and looked around. He was in a hospital room. His wife sat next to him, smiling and holding his hand. The police asked a few questions and then left to let him rest. They said they would be back in a few days when they would want to talk more. They posted extra policemen just outside his room.

A few days later they did return. Simon described to them what happened and gave a description of the man who headed the group and what he called himself. The police found and arrested the boss based on Simon's description. The newspapers ran headline after headline about what happened and had Simon's picture on the front page for days.

Simon, reading some of the articles, found out that the man he described was the head of a large underworld crime syndicate. He was upset that anyone got out of the store alive and threatened to correct the oversight. Simon was frightened. His wife and daughter visited daily and the police remained outside his hospital room.

The Attorney General came to visit Simon. He asked for his testimony at the trial. Simon asked how he would be able to return to his normal life. The attorney said that this was no longer possible. Simon asked what would happen after the trial. He was not only worried about himself but there were now also threats against his family.

The attorney could come up with only one solution. They could place Simon in the witness protection program. However, if the whole family disappeared, as strong as the boss was, he would continue to look. They had a plan. They would fake Simon's death. He could be moved to another location and given a new identity. His family though would have to stay and could not be told of the deception.

Simon wrestled with this plan. He did not want to live without his wife and daughter, yet it seemed that this was the only way they could have a life. Simon was crushed. He decided that the course of action suggested by the police was the only possible choice. He would never be able to see his daughter again.

The trial went as planned. Simon testified, the boss was convicted and sentenced to life in prison without parole. On hearing the verdict he turned toward Simon and said that he would get him. Simon said that he already had. On leaving the courthouse Simon entered a car and it slowly began to drive off. Simon exited the car through a trap door in the car floor and dropped into a manhole underneath, just before the car began to move. The car exploded a block from the courthouse. The papers reported the next day that Simon had been killed in the explosion.

Simon was whisked away by Federal agents to a spot unknown and set up with a new life. He could never contact his family and his heart ached. Simon placed the boss in jail but Simon was also convicted with the same sentence, even though he had committed no crime. He failed at holding down any new job that the government arranged for. He finally decided to join a circus and travel around the country. They had openings for a clown and he signed up. It was not a good life but the movement seemed to sooth him.

Ten years passed. The papers reported that the crime boss had died in jail. Simon wondered if he could now try and reach his family but did not know how or what to do. His wife may have remarried and his daughter would now be grown. She probably would not even remember him.

The circus was due to perform in his old hometown. He decided to see if they were still there. They were. His wife did remarry. His daughter was now a junior in High School. He still did not know if he should try and talk with them or how it might disrupt their lives. He decided not to call but he just had to see his daughter, even if it were for just a moment. He had a letter dropped off at their house. The card inside said that they had won a contest and received two free admissions to the circus, with the tickets enclosed.

The day arrived for the performance. Simon followed his usual routine and placed on his face makeup and clown suit. As the crowd began to enter the tent for the performance, he looked toward the seats that corresponded to the tickets he sent. Mother and daughter filled his tearful sight as Simon's heart raced uncontrollably.

As the show continued he could not take his eyes off the seats. He felt excited, angry, and happy. Every emotion waved through his body. During the finale, the clowns were to scatter throughout the tent. Simon jumped a barrier and began to climb the stairs to where his former wife and daughter sat. As he made his way next to their seats they looked up but did not recognize him in any way.

Tears started to stream down the clown's face and smear his makeup. The daughter asked her mother why the clown was crying. The mother responded that she did not know. Simon reached into his costume and pulled out a tattered book. He handed it to the daughter. The pages were worn with wear to the point that the book was barely holding together. Looking at the front, the cloud formations spread over the cover were barely visible. Inside the clouds the cows, grain and people were badly faded and looked ghost like. The upper smeared title could barely been seen. It said "Dreamland".

The daughter holding the book with both hands, slowly looked up at the clown...Daddy? Simon, now crying uncontrollably, nodded his head. His daughter jumped up and hugged him, squeezing so hard it took the breath from him. The wife fainted outright.

Simon moved back to the city. He would not interfere with his wife's new family. That would not be fair to her or her new husband. The years had placed a barrier between them that would not be breached. Yet he could visit and be with his daughter. They talked almost every day by telephone and met every Friday night. They would meet for dinner, conversation and a night out. As they said goodbye for the evening they would always speak the words of that little book, hug each other and say "I love you".

Midrash Vayechi
The Twelve Blessings

Linda was a doctor. Not just any doctor but a specialist in children with cancer. She saw the worst of the worst, children with cases that limited their chances of survival to only a few months. It placed stress on a person that was hard to measure. Yet Linda knew that someone had to help these children and she did as much as she could for these unfortunate souls. After her rounds she would sit with the kids and read a story. Linda would animate her voice imitating the characters. The kids seemed to love it and it always put a smile on their face.

It was mid-December and with the hospital located in upper Minnesota, the weather was snowy and cold. Most people left for end of year vacations and to be with their families for the holidays. Linda had not married. Her mother and father died years ago. There were no brothers or sisters and what extended family there was had not stayed in contact. She did not quite know what she would do with her time off.

Linda began to make rounds through the hospital. There were twelve patients in the children's cancer ward. She went bed to bed meeting with each child, doing what she does best, and, as always, finished with a story read to all the children.

At day's end Linda headed out the front of the hospital to go home. A car swung up the circular drive and did not see Linda enter the driveway. It clipped her side. Linda flew through the air landing in a snow bank. Hospital personnel saw the accident, rushed out to Linda and carefully moved her back into the hospital.

The car had broken her leg, her arm and smashed a few ribs. Her face was bruised and cut. The doctors did not find any internal bleeding but felt Linda might also have a concussion. They placed her in a hospital bed and told her she would need to stay there for a least a week. They gave her an entire ward as most of the patients had been sent home for the holidays.

Linda, depressed, cried the night away. The dark dreary season, the loneliness, her patients, all just seemed to overtake her physically wracked body. The next day Linda remained in her bed dozing, drifting and feeling very sorry for herself. Her mood fit the drabness viewed through the window.

Linda noticed one of the swinging doors to the
wardroom open. From her position in bed she could only view
the topside of the door and saw no-one enter. Yet she could
hear sounds of wheels turning against the floor. Suddenly there
was a crash against her bed. Linda swung her body over to the
side of the bed and viewed a child below. One of her cancer
kids had snuck onto a small-wheeled gurney and rolled herself
into her wardroom.

The child, all smiles, grabbed the side of the bed and
swung herself up. She held a package of marking pens in her
mouth. Child number one asked if she could draw pictures on
Linda's casts. Linda smiled and said it was fine. For the next
hour they talked and the child drew on both the arm and leg
cast. There were no words or figures to speak of, only different
colored shapes that intermingled with each other. It was
actually quite beautiful and seemed to lighten up the whole
room.

As the child was about to finish her drawing, the doors
of the ward squeaked open a second time. Two other cancer
children entered with paper grocery bags. They giggled as they
entered. The children said that the color of the casts did not
match the room. They began to toss colored streamers up in
the air. The ribbons hooked through the exposed rafters
above. Soon the room looked like a New Year's Eve Party.

As the ribbons were hurled throughout the room, the
door popped open again. A fourth cancer child entered with a
CD player. She set it up, plugged it in and started playing
music. It was an instrumental that Linda had not heard. Music
filled the air and penetrated her body, soothing and relaxing
her tense muscles.

Cancer child five, six and seven suddenly entered the room, each holding a tray of food. There were cakes and candy and fruits of all types and flavors. Linda tried to ask where they got such a variety and all the kids did was smile.

Without a second thought cancer child eight and nine popped in. They had already decorated themselves with ribbons, bows and sparkly stars over their drab hospital gowns. The kids went from child to child placing colorful twinkling objects all over their clothes. They also helped Linda decorate her gown as well.

Linda wondered how far this might go when cancer children ten and eleven entered. They had taken the fruit drinks that they normally receive and added some seven-up to give it fizz. Each flavor had its own bowl. The kids froze some ice in special animal trays they found and dumped the iced animals into the bowls. Looking onto the top of the bowls you could see bobbing bears, elephants and lions, moving up and down in the fizzing liquid. A smile came over Linda's face.

One of the kids moved to the end of the room and shut off the lights, while others lit candles all around. The door opened for a last time. Cancer child number twelve entered in a wheelchair and stopped next to Linda's bed. In her lap a story book. Linda lifted the book up to read. The children all gathered around, over and under Linda's bed. It was as if she had children draped everywhere. The book was full of short stories about different animals. As she read and came to a new animal one of the children would make the sound of that animal in the background.

Suddenly the lights flickered on. The nurses had found the party and started to break it up. As each child was roused from Linda's bed they gave her a hug, a kiss and a broad smile. The smile was infectious. It went from the child to Linda, and her smile grew as each of the twelve touched her.

Linda could not sleep. Thoughts of these cancer stricken children and their exuberance for life made her mind race. She could not take the smile off her face. These kids, most of who would not see past another month, had given her a gift she would never forget. To them it was not so much how a person dies but how a person lives, that mattered. They would enjoy whatever time they had, in whatever way they could. Linda, a person with so much time, focused on death and the depression that was around her. These children, who knew death intimately, chose to smile, be happy and celebrate life.

The next morning Linda had to get out of bed. A nurse helped her into a wheelchair and together traveled to the children's cancer ward. As they entered the room the kids all cheered and jumped out of their beds to race to her side. Linda, still all smiles, lifted a book from her lap and began to read...

Midrash Shemot
The Thornbush

Sarah's teacher announced to the class that they would be having their own Science Fair this year. The class was divided into two sections, animal and plant. Sarah ended up in the plant group. The teacher wrote a number of plant names on pieces of paper and placed them into a hat. Each student was to pick a piece of paper and that was the plant they were to work with for the Class Science Fair. The first student picked the piece of paper with the name rose bush, the second student picked sunflowers, and a third picked a small elm tree. Then it was Sarah's turn. She picked the piece of paper out of the hat and unrolled it. It said thorn bush.

As she heard the picks of the other students, Sarah became depressed. There were interesting animals, birds, pretty flowers and even full-grown trees. The one she would have liked the most was the small hummingbird that went to the student who sat next to her. All were far more interesting than her choice. She asked the teacher to please let her pick another choice or give this plant to someone else who might want it. The teacher refused and said that she was to make the best of it. Reluctantly Sarah agreed.

All the plants and animals were placed in a staged area adjacent to the school and next to a small grove of woods. The class went to examine their choices. The closer Sarah got to the thorn bush the uglier it became. The more she looked at it, the more she longed not to have any part of this schrub. There was no redeeming value she could see. The branches skewed in every direction. They were gnarled and kinked. Not one speck of green foliage sprouted from this plant. Along the branches thorns bulged out in absolute randomness, pointed and dangerous. After this first encounter Sarah again asked the teacher to choose someone else to do the thorn bush. The teacher refused and stated that Sarah would need to accept the fact that it was her job.

At this point Sarah decided to simply make the best of it. She researched the thorn bush and found out everything she could about this plant. How it grows best, the soil it likes, and how to prune such a plant. She also searched for any piece of trivia that could make her paper more interesting. She wrote a whole chapter on the subject of the thorn bush in the Bible.

Sarah placed proper minerals and what she called plant food in and around the bush to try and make it as strong as possible. She noticed how her classmates seemed so happy to be working with the plants and animals they chose. The students would often tease Sarah about the thorn bush. They said that Sarah should be kind and just kill it. The harder they laughed the more resolute Sarah became to protect it.

Over the next few months each of the students grew, groomed and took care of their respective plant or animal. The thorn bush did not grow much but the branches and roots seemed thicker and stronger. The following week was to be the final showing for the Class Science Fair. All the other plants and animals seemed so much brighter and prettier. Yet Sarah had a newfound respect for this plant. Although it was not nice to look at, it was healthy and in excellent shape. Sarah headed home and would wait for the judgment to come the next day, when the teacher would grade their projects.

As night fell, the winds began to pick up. The news said that bad storms were about to hit the area and all should take cover. The rains began and then the most horrendous lightning cracked through the air. The heaven was constantly lit as one bolt after another moved across the night sky.

A bulletin moved appeared on the bottom of the television screen. The woods next to the school had caught on fire because of the lightning. Firefighters were on their way and the public was warned to stay away from the area. Sarah became just like a worried mother. She prayed that nothing would happen to her thorn bush. She strained to catch a view as the television cameras scanned the school and then the woods. It was just too dark to see anything but the firefighters as they scurried from one flame to another.

The school was closed the next day because of the damage to the adjacent woods. The firemen were still putting out the last of the flames and the area was barricaded so no-one could come close. But there was no question as to what happened. The entire project area had been burned. The enclosure the animals were in was nothing but a pile of mangled wire and ashes. The animals and birds were gone. The flowers and trees that the students worked on were scarred and ripped apart.

Sarah noticed her thorn bush. Although not shredded like the other plants, it was charred and burned. Black soot covered its gnarled branches. Sarah felt a tear roll down her cheek. She remembered the word holocaust. The Holocaust was the murder of six million Jews during World War II by the Nazis but came from the Greek, meaning destruction by fire. The word resonated deep within her. She turned and went home.

School was not back in session for another week. On their return the teacher said that she wanted the class to go to the project area. The class, heartbroken, did not really want to but the teacher insisted. The area still had barricades up, making it impossible to get close. From a distance, however, some of the details could be made out and what became visible was most amazing.

The thorn bush had been washed off by the rains of the last few days. It was alive and well. In its center was the small hummingbird. It had escaped the fire and returned to make a nest in the center of the bush. Through the branches on the ground a chipmunk was seen. It had burrowed from below and was using the bush for protection. And even the thorn bush had now sprouted a few small green leaves scattered around the branches, giving color and beauty against the burnt forest. It wasn't the majestic trees or beautiful animals that centered the revival for these woods, but a simple thorn bush.

Midrash Vaera
To Find My Name

      I woke to find myself in a place I did not know. My hands reached for my head only to find a bandage tightly wrapped, totally encompassing my skull. It took a few minutes for my eyes to focus. When they did, tubes, IV bottles and a myriad of medical equipment became visible. I was in a hospital.

68

A doctor entered and saw that my eyes were opened. He asked how I felt. I honestly did not know how to answer. He informed me that I had been hit by a runaway car while crossing a street. Physically I had a few broken bones but other than that everything else checked out.

A person seeing the accident said that as I tumbled from the impact with the car my head snapped back and hit the pavement pretty hard. The doctor said he would ask a series of questions to determine if there might be a problem with my brain. He said he would start with the easiest. What was my name? I told the doctor he needn't go any further. I had not the slightest idea what my name was!

The doctor left and returned with a number of colleagues. They asked if I could remember anything about my life. Quite simply I had no idea who I was! I could not remember any detail, large or small, about my life. The doctors indicated that it was probably a temporary situation as they could find no physical damage to the brain. The method of treatment would be to slowly introduce me to other people in my life and hopefully that would jog my memory to return.

A few hours passed and the only interruptions were from the nurses who would now and then check the various tubes poked into my body. Then a handsome lady entered. As she saw me her hands raised to cover her mouth which had let out a rather audible gasp. Tears began to well up in her eyes. I just laid there not knowing quite what to do or say. After composing herself she came over and gave me a light kiss on the cheek. I envisioned a cloud inside my head and it began to dissipate. On clearing, a word appeared... and it spelled husband!

We talked for a while. In time I even remembered her name. Yet it was strange. I could still not remember my own. I asked her to please tell me because it was very embarrassing. She said the doctors asked her not to reveal my name, as I needed to remember that on my own.

A bit later two small children entered the hospital room. The cloud returned inside my head and again dissipated. On clearing, another word appeared...it spelled father! The kids jumped onto the bed and each gave me a big hug and kiss. A small tear trickled down my face. I did not know why I felt this great internal emotion. All the same, the tear trickled down. I was hoping that the kids would somehow slip and let out my name. But no, they only called me father or dad.

The doctors let me get out of bed and my wife helped me take a few steps down the hall. An older woman exited the hospital elevator. As she saw me she shrieked in joy and began to run toward me. The cloud again formed inside my head and disappeared revealing the word...son! My wife told my mother about the name problem and asked her not to tell. We talked for a while and my mother left with my children.

I returned to bed and slept for a few hours. I awoke when a man noisily opened my room door. He held a book and some paper in his hands. The cloud returned and again dissipated to reveal... teacher. The man was the principal at the school where I worked. He was warned, like the others, not to reveal my name and unfortunately complied with the request. He gave me the book which was signed by all my students wishing me a speedy recovery. The paper was for me to use as I saw fit. He said that I should take it easy for a while and when I was ready, I could return to my job.

As time passed other names revealed themselves. I was an American, a citizen of the United States. I was an amateur chess player, a weekend golfer, a Jew! I was chairman of a local charity, a collector of rare manuscripts, and I also was a teacher at the local community college. So many names, each describing a part of my life, yet I still could not remember my given name.

This was certainly frustrating. But it was all the more so because nobody else would say it! I sat up in my bed and grabbed the writing paper from the nightstand that the principal brought. Even the paper seemed frustrated as it had curled up like a scroll. I rolled it out and used the book at the top to hold it open.

I began to just doodle around the page with some crayons that my children left. I picked up the black one and made some abstract marks which turned into a cloud looking structure. I placed the black one down and picked up a white crayon. My hand moved across the cloud, as if a power not my own dictated the movement. Letters began to form. When my hand stopped, a name appeared centered within the black cloud. It spelled Moshe...

Midrash Bo
The Baker

There were certain privileges in being a freelance newspaper reporter. One of them was to travel the city and discover people and places that seem hidden from the rest of the population. It was on one of those excursions that I discovered a bakery whose products could only be described as heaven on earth. It was tucked away in a rundown neighborhood of the inner city.

The owner, and sole proprietor, was an elderly portly looking gentleman. He looked scuffled and disheveled. Yet his bread was ambrosia to the taste, and always caused a smile to appear.

Every Friday, for the past five years, I would stop for a loaf of his freshly baked bread. The store itself was in the center of a block, surrounded by broken and burned buildings. The baker's father opened the shop some years ago, when the neighborhood was alive and vibrant. The son took over the business when the father became sick and eventually passed away. As the years rolled on, the neighborhood continued to decay. The son simply never moved away.

Week after week I purchased from the baker. Yet I never took time to talk with him. He was not very sociable but also did not seem mean or unfriendly. He just kept his distance. Perhaps he was comfortable in his isolation. In retrospect it seems strange that a newspaper person would not be inquisitive enough to investigate a true gem in the middle of all this rubble.

It was Friday again, and I slipped away from the office to go and purchase my weekly loaf. When I arrived, the store was closed up tight. A note was pinned to the door. The baker died the night before. As I stood in remorse, feeling sorry that I could no longer savor this special bread, a lady walked up to the door and gasped at the note.

I inquired as to who she was. She said she ran the homeless shelter down the street. The baker had always brought food every Friday for anyone staying at the shelter. She worried when she did not see him at his normal time and came to see if he was all right. I said, "You mean he brought a few loaves of bread to the shelter". She said, "No, he purchased groceries for all the homeless that stayed with them that day". As word spread that there was always food at the shelter on Friday. Basically anyone in need would show up at our doorstep on that day. The baker never disappointed by being short of food and he never asked a thing from anyone at the shelter.

The woman turned to return to her post and a few kids on bicycles rode up to the building. They could not have been much more than ten years old. On seeing the note they sat down on the side of the curb and had the most forlorn look on their faces. I asked if they knew the baker. They said yes and proceeded to tell me that the baker helped them with their schoolwork. I ask them to explain. He said, "He would pay them each a dollar just to go to school. They had to prove to him that they were there that day to get the money and he took time to help them with their homework. If they did well on tests he would give prizes."

As a reporter I was stunned that this man seemed to mean so much to others and I had no idea what was going on. I wondered how many others this man helped. I decided to use my influence at the paper to try to find out. I wrote a piece that the editor placed on the front page. The funeral for the baker was to be in three days, allowing for the only living relative, a brother, to make it into town. I asked in the article that anyone who was helped by this man, might honor him by showing up at the funeral, and I gave the details.

I decided to leave for the funeral early. I thought it may have been a little too early and saw a group of kids playing basketball in back of one of the schools. I pulled into the lot to watch awhile. A beautiful park rimmed with flowers, picnic benches, and playground equipment surrounded the court. My sight focused on a small sign on one of the fences. The unpretentious sign simply said that the baker donated the park and all the equipment.

The funeral service was to take place in a large one-room building at the cemetery. I arrived early and introduced myself to the brother. The brother said it was nice of me to print the article and asked me and a few from the homeless shelter to act as pallbearers. I was wondering what affect the article might have and worried that maybe I built this man's image up in my own mind. As time moved closer to the start of the funeral, the room continued to fill, until not another soul could fit in. I could see others milling outside, not able to fit into this structure.

I went over to a group of kids that took up three whole rows. They were in hockey jerseys. The coach told me that the baker had paid for all the uniforms and equipment for the team for many years.

An older gentleman in a baker's hat made his way into the building. He came over to me and told me all the bakers in the city had gathered and would wait outside to give their compatriot a final honor. I asked why they would do such a thing. He said, "Some years ago there was a major flood that hit the city and the bakers could not receive the bulk wheat that was needed. The deceased baker not only arranged for transport of his own needs but took care of all his competitors, citywide. He took nothing extra for himself and diverted a big problem for people of the city that needed this food".

I could not believe what I was hearing. A man who melded into the city, nondescript, hidden from view, for years made such a major impact on so many lives. The brother started to give a eulogy but decided to have others around the room share how the baker had made such a positive difference in their lives. There were no tears at this funeral. This was a celebration of a man, a mensch, someone who lived by the principles he believed in.

As the last person spoke, we picked up the coffin and began to move it to the burial plot outside. It was difficult to move, as there was not a spot in the room not occupied. The standing room crowd turned as the coffin passed, in respect. As we exited the building, I was at first blinded by the sunlight. I felt the presence of others but could not quite make out the blurred shifting environment around me. Then my eyes settled and refocused. For as far as my eyes could see... people. Thousands came to pay their respects.

This man had touched so many. The bakers filtered through the crowd and handed everyone they could reach something I could not quite make out. As the casket passed, the people in the crowd raised their hands in the air. In their grasp, a small piece of unleavened bread, matzah- a sea of matzah, a final honor from a city to a baker.

Midrash Beshalach
Arms of Support

Ari was but a teenager, growing up in Israel. Like his
friends, he was doing a tour of duty in the army. What made
Ari different was his meticulous, methodical focus on keeping
the best physique a person could have. Everything about his
life led in one way or another toward molding and keeping a
strong, well-tuned body.

Ari's physical prowess allowed him to be part of a special corp. The group would travel in difficult areas that were inaccessible by machinery. Often times that meant bombed out buildings or ravaged sections of cities.

Ari's group consisted of twelve men. Each man had a specialty but their main call to fame was working as a group. The men, including Ari, was led by the eldest of the military unit, a thirty-five year old mustached, hard-as-nails commander, named Joshua. Joshua led by example and through the use of simple hand gestures could communicate to his troop exactly what he required.

The unit was asked to enter a small village on the border of the West Bank. It was an unusual place in that both Israelis and Palestinians lived side by side. This made the area turbulent and explosive. The previous day mortar and gunfire destroyed many buildings. Ari's group was sent to assess the damage.

The morning went reasonably well. The troop made a methodical search street by street, building by broken building. For the most part the structures were empty. They came across an occasional resident who had a few cuts or scrapes, but nothing that required hospitalization.

They decided to move to a neighboring street where the buildings were not quite so damaged. The first structure had a sidewall blown out but the remainder seemed fine. As they moved searching through the structure, they heard screams just outside. Rifle shots pierced the air along with shouts of Arabic.

78

Ari peeked over a window and saw a masked terrorist shoving and rounding up people in the adjacent square. He used his gun like a staff, herding the people toward their building. As the masked man entered, the military unit began to close around him, silently, undetected.

The terrorist moved the people down a flight of stairs into a cellar. As he turned the unit could see an interior jacket within his robe filled with explosives. He placed his hands inside a large hole in the wall and removed a large white round object, the size of a basketball. He moved to the stairwell door, smiled, spoke a few Arabic words and tossed the object into the air.

As the object hurled skyward a shot rang out hitting the terrorist directly in the center of the forehead. He dropped like a limp rag. Ari, in a reflex action, jumped at the tossed object. He caught it midair, arms stretched out, hitting the ground softly, deftly, directly in the middle of the stairwell door.

Instinctively he did not make a move. Sprawled on his back, his arms stretched straight out, the white object was held aloft. Joshua approached quickly screaming to Ari not to move. The devise he caught was a bomb. His hand held in a button on a device that if he let go would explode. Ari obeyed.

Quickly Joshua communicated with his headquarters. The device Ari so gingerly held was a new type of bomb. Only a few people in the army knew how to disarm it safely. Headquarters would get someone there as soon as they could but it might be hours before someone would arrive. It was critical that Ari not move. If he tried to get up the bomb would go off.

Joshua moved the military unit and anyone else he could out of the building. He assessed the situation. The people in the cellar were trapped. There was no second exit. With Ari blocking the door they could not move out through the stairwell. A secondary problem was that Ari had fallen onto the terrorist. If he dropped the bomb, it would also set off the explosives that were on his body. The combination would most certainly kill all the people in the cellar.

The last bad news was that although Ari was as strong as they come, he was laying with his arms stretched out. There would be no way for him to remain in that position for the length of time it took for someone to get there to defuse the bomb.

Word had spread through the neighborhood and a crowd was gathering around the building. Joshua had the military unit isolate the area and act as a barricade to prevent others from wandering into the building. A camera was placed just inside the door so Joshua and others could monitor the situation safely. This also gave the public view of what was going on. It seemed like only minutes passed when television and radio crews also gathered at the site.

Time passed. A normal person would not be able to hold Ari's position for more than twenty minutes. It was now two hours. As strong as Ari was, sweat began to stream down his face and his arms began to slightly quiver.

Two unit members, seeing Ari's situation, bolted for the building. They moved quickly to Ari's side and locked their hands around each of Ari's arms, like a homemade splint. The supporting action immobilized Ari's arms. He would be able to hold the bomb aloft with their assistance.

The action of the two unit members created a secondary problem. The helpers also had their arms extended. Unlike Ari, they would be able to hold for only fifteen to twenty minutes. As that time frame approached, two other unit members moved inside the building and took their place. From that point on, every fifteen minutes, the two unit members inside were relieved by two others who helped lock Ari's arms motionless, held high in the air.

Ari trying to take his mind off his situation, talked with the people caught in the cellar. He explained the predicament to them as best he could. The people in the cellar looked for anything that might help them either escape or at the very least protect themselves from the possible explosion, but there was no place to exit and nothing but bare walls in the dank cellar.

There were twenty people trapped. What was unusual was that it was a combination of Israelis and Palestinians. The terrorist in his vehemence did not bother to ask affiliation. His mind was on one task, to blow up as many people as he could. Although his fight was supposed to be directed against the Israelis, his own mind was blinded by the very terrorism he sought to wreak on his enemies. Ari had a similar single directed outlook. It did not matter to him if the people in the cellar were Jews or Muslims or anything else for that matter. They were simply people and to him they had a right to live.

It began to turn dusk when the army expert finally showed up. He moved inside the building to the bomb held high by Ari. He joked that this was the first time he had a chance to work on a bomb that was set so nicely for him. Normally it was jammed into a corner or some inaccessible location. He thanked Ari.

It took the expert about twenty more minutes to defuse the white object. He took it from Ari and gently moved it outside to an isolated area where it was blown up safely, away from any person. The same was done with the explosives the terrorist had on his body.

As the bomb was taken from Ari, the supporting unit members also released their locking hands. Ari's arms dropped to his sides. He had no feeling in them at all. It was as if they were not even connected to his body. Assisted up he took a few steps and sat on an adjacent chair next to the doorway. His arms dangled to his sides, rubber like, limp and at this point unusable.

As the people exited the cellar, they passed Ari. Each thanked him in their own way. It might have been a hug, a kiss on the cheek or a simple thank you. One Palestinian stopped in front of Ari and respectfully nodded his head. As the last person from the cellar exited the building, a few unit members helped Ari up and began to walk out of the building.

Although it was the dead of night when they left the structure, it seemed as if it was midday. The television crews had set up their lights and there were so many and so strong, it made it seem like day. The lights and so many people surrounding the building shocked Ari and his fellow soldiers to a standstill.

The crowd grew quiet as the twelve-man military unit came together in the center of the square. Not a sound was heard. Someone in the front of the crowd raised both hands in the air, mimicking the position that Ari held the bomb in. Other people in the crowd began to do the same. As arms were raised they would join hands with the person next to them.

It was an eerie wonderful scene. The entire block filled with people, hands raised in the air, joined with their neighbor. The military unit, gathered together, helped raise Ari's arms and mimicked what the crowd was doing. As they placed their hands up in the air, the crowd screamed in delight. Joshua scanned the crowd. It was not Israelis or Palestinians, Muslims or Jews...but just people.

Midrash Yitro
A Conversation

Every Friday, after school, I picked up my granddaughter and we would go to the park. She would play with her friends, we would grab something to eat from the resident vendors, we would walk, and we always had conversations. Those talks never took the form found between normal people. It was more of a game. We always went off in directions that were bizarre and unique.

I enjoyed sitting on a bench adjacent to the playground equipment. It was surrounded by majestic green trees, and had a perfect view so I could see my granddaughter romp to her heart's content. After releasing her pent up energy from sitting in school all day, she would come sit next to me on this bench, and the conversation would begin...

Nechdah (Hebrew for granddaughter): "Saba, see those people at the bus stop over there. Do you recognize them?"

Saba (Hebrew for grandfather): "I certainly do Nechdah!"

Nechdah: "See the man with the blue necktie?"

Saba: "Yes."

Nechdah: "His name is You Shall Not Murder." A smile broached the granddaughter's face.

Saba: "Tell me more, Nechdah!"

Nechdah: "Do Not Murder is famous in our town. He once saved the mayor of our city. A man with a gun ran at the mayor when he was giving a speech. Do Not Murder jumped in front of the mayor and took the bullet instead. The gunshot hit him in the shoulder. That is why he leans against the bus stop pole the way he does."

Saba: "Nechdah, I know the man next to Do Not Murder, it is You Shall Not Steal! His picture was in the newspaper the other day. He helped the police stop a robbery at the Jewelry Store downtown."

Nechdah: "Saba, next to You Shall Not Steal is an old friend of mine, You Shall Not Covet Your Neighbor's Things. He lives in the house next to me. He has the best baseball glove in the whole neighborhood. My brother was always talking about it. I talked with father and he gave my brother a baseball glove for Hanukkah but I think my brother still likes Covet's better."

Saba: "Nechdah, do you see the lady in the green dress at the other end of the bus stop? She is the best artist in the entire city, and people all over the world know her work. I heard some crazy man broke into her store the other night and broke all her sculptures. But I cannot remember her name. Do you know who she is?"

Nechdah: "I certainly do, it is You Shall Have No Other Gods Beside Me."

Saba: "Oh, now I remember! Have you read about the big court case? Next to the artist is the famous lawyer, You Shall Not Bear False Witness. I heard he caught one of the witnesses making up a story about the person on trial."

Nechdah: "Saba, is that the truth?"

Saba: "I cannot Swear To God! No, wait, he is standing next to You Shall Not Bear False Witness!"

Nechdah: "Saba, do you see the little girl in the middle? She is in one of my classes at school. Her name is You Shall Never Commit to Be an Adult. Something happened between the parents. I heard that the father came home one day and found some other man in the house. I don't understand, but the parents are getting a divorce and she is moving out of the city to live with her grandparents."

Saba: "That is very sad, Nechdah. I thought her name was You shall Never Commit Adultery, but perhaps you are right about her name. I understand your mother is going to make a wonderful dinner tonight, so we should not eat too many snacks. When your mother was your age she always loved Friday nights and would make a big deal of it. Because of this her friends gave her a nickname, Remember The Sabbath, and it stuck ever since."

Nechdah: "Saba, can we walk home now so we will not be late for our Shabbat meal?"

Saba: "Well, I may not be the Lord Your God, but I think I know the way home. I only need one more thing... Do you know what it is?"

Nechdah sat in great thought for a few moments. You could see her thinking, counting with her fingers and mumbling some words. Finally, her face lit up and she stood on top of the park bench so she could be next to the face of her grandfather.

Nechdah: "I remembered something my parents wanted me do for them. They asked me to find their friend at the park. His name is Honor Your Father and Mother. They asked me to give him something."

Saba: "And what pray tell what might that be Nechdah?" A big smile came over her face. She leaned over and kissed Saba on the cheek. He smiled at her, took her hand and said, "Shabbat Shalom, let's go home."

Midrash Mishpatim
An Eye for an Eye

Jacob was the head of a large manufacturing corporation. The company made a variety of small parts used in the construction of an automobile. The plant had smelters, molding machines, presses and most anything that could be used to make some of the finest auto parts in the world.

As efficient and successful as the company was, Jacob was also known for a hobby. He loved flowers. More specifically he loved to breed new flowers. Of all the flowers he created, his pride and joy was a new kind of iris. It was spectacular. The outer petals were a deep violet. So deep was the color that it made a person feel like they were lost in a deep dark canyon, where no light could ever penetrate. The center of the flower contained a spot that resembled the sun. The yellow center was so bright it hurt to look at it. At the border, where the yellow met the purple, was like staring at a sunrise- that part of the morning when it was not quite fully dark nor when light was truly discernable.

What was strange about this flower was, try as he might, he could never quite reproduce its beauty in any other flower he tried to grow. It was a one of a kind. It won every show he entered it in and stamped his reputation as a genius. This flower was unique. It even had its own name. It was called "Eye of the Sun". The trade magazines and papers shortened it to "The Eye".

At a company staff meeting one of the foremen brought up some issues with the stamping equipment. It seemed as if the lubrication systems were beginning to fail. As they were heading into the end of the year rush, Jacob decided to hold off repairs until the Holiday break.

Evan was a stamping machine operator. He had worked this job some ten years and though it was not very exciting, it was steady and allowed him to make a living for his family. He lived with his wife and two children in a small house at the edge of town. It was not much to look at, but it was home for him. It was Evan and his co-workers who had told the foreman of the system problems. They trusted the company would take care of the issue.

On the last day of work before the holiday break, the lubrication hoses on the machine that Evan worked at blew under the pressure of the stamping action. Hot oil sprayed everywhere. The spray showered Evan's head and he fell screaming to the floor. He was rushed to the hospital. The doctors treated the burns on his head from the hot lubricant. They flushed out both his eyes but one was so badly burned it could not be saved. Evan laid quietly in a dark hospital room.

Jacob was devastated when he heard the news. He paced the evening away wondering how his employee was faring. Jacob went to the hospital the next day but Evan would not allow any visitors. Part of Evan felt sad. The doctor said that his eye could never be repaired. Part of him was mad. Why didn't the company fix the problem when it was brought to their attention?

Evan finally allowed visitors and Jacob was one of the first to enter the room. He apologized for the accident and said that the company would take care of things. Now more upset than hurt, Evan said that it would take more than an apology to compensate for what happened. Evan knew the value that the president placed on his flower. He said not only would the company pay his medical expenses and provide a job he could do with one eye, but he also wanted his prized flower. Evan wanted an eye for an eye. Jacob was dumbfounded. Of all the unexpected requests, he never anticipated this. Without saying another word Jacob left the hospital.

    A few weeks later Evan was sent home to finish
recuperating. Jacob pondered the request. That iris was his
most prized possession. Yet it was his decision that led to the
accident that caused his employee to lose his eye. How can
one place a price on an eye? A few days later Jacob went to
Evan's house and gave him the flower. No words were
exchanged. He simply entered the house, handed him the
potted plant, turned and walked back out of the house.

    Evan never expected the president to turn over the
flower. The request was made out of anger. Yet he took it and
knew he would not give it back. He pondered. Should he
simply destroy this iris, like his own eye had been destroyed?
He looked at it and even with one eye, knew that to tear it up
was wrong. He turned to his wife and told her to plant it in
their garden outside. It was not really a garden, more like a
collection of weeds. Evan felt that with winter approaching,
Mother Nature would take its own toll on the one of a kind
flower.

    Time passed, and the fall winds blew the leaves off the
trees. The green vegetation turned brown and slowly withered
away as winter set in. The iris disappeared under a blanket of
snow. Evan returned to work as an employee representative.
He could no longer work on the machines with only one eye.
He did not like this new job but what else could he do. He
had to work to make a living.

    As spring burst upon the scene a reporter for one of
the flower journals paid a visit to Jacob. He was there to do a
story on his famous iris. Jacob told him he no longer
possessed it, told him the story of what happened and sadly
slipped out of the room. The reporter tracked down Evan at
the plant and asked him what he did with the flower. Evan
explained and said that surely it no longer existed on this earth.

Out of curiosity the reporter asked if Evan would mind showing him what he called the weed garden. As they drove to Evan's house the reporter noticed the wet pavement and fields. The water created a unique smell of spring. They walked to the back of Evan's yard and saw the place where Evan's wife had planted it. The ground was covered with weeds and there was no sign of the iris.

It was so sad to believe that the most famous flower in the world had died such an ignominious death. As the reporter scratched the ground looking for evidence of the famous iris, Evan turned toward an overgrown field about fifty yards in back of the house. He spotted a curious mixture of color splashed at various points across the ground. He walked over to the field and saw small wildflowers poking from beneath the surface. Brushing some of the dirt away he noticed a few of the flowers had small petals with that same dark purple of the famous iris. Next to it was another flower with a yellow center. Though still very small, the flower contained that same bright yellow that distinguished the famous iris.

Evan carefully gathered a few samples of the wildflowers in some pots and had the reporter drive him back to the plant. They were in the middle of a staff meeting when he strolled right into Jacob's office. Evan walked over to Jacob and placed the fragile wildflowers on the table in front of him. A smile crept over Jacob's face.

Evan and Jacob went together to the field in back of Evan's house. They gathered many of flowers. Together with the reporter they documented their find. Jacob had tried to cultivate the iris with other pure bread species but it did not take. It needed something wild to cross-fertilize with.

Jacob taught Evan all about flowers and together they opened a small horticulture establishment, centered on the wildflowers. They called the new business Eye of the Sun, after the mother of their most famous product. Evan found joy in this new career, the flowers, a friendship and a new life. Jacob felt like a weight had been lifted off his shoulders. As important as the iris was to him, the fact that his decision had badly hurt another person left an indelible mark on his soul. That Jacob could teach Evan about flowers, and the joy he had received from that one iris that had now multiplied into thousands, seemed to redeem him. Evan and Jacob prospered together.

Midrash Terumah
Menorah Man

Joshua made a living as a scrap recycler. He would travel in his truck to various building demolition jobs around the city, pick up metals like copper, nickel, stainless steel and any other nonferrous metals he could find. He brought them in, segregated them, cleaned them, and then sold them to foundries, which smelted them down for reuse.

Early in his career one of the synagogues in town was vandalized and burned to the ground. He went there, sifted through the wreckage, and found a small brass menorah. It was twisted and charred. He showed it to the rabbi who told Joshua to keep it. It was so mangled that it would be of no further use.

Joshua took the menorah back home and over the next several days, worked to see if he could fix the distorted artifact. He pried and tapped and bent and used every tool he owned to try to repair the menorah. Slowly it seemed to retake its shape. Joshua buffed and polished and rubbed and shined the piece until any remnant of its dilapidated condition was no longer visible. The seven-stemmed Jewish candleholder seemed to have a new inner glow that radiated to the surrounding space.

Joshua placed the menorah on top of the cab of his collection truck. As he drove around the city, it shown like a beacon for anyone who cared to look. People around the city began to call him by a new nickname, the Menorah Man!

The menorah did not help much in getting new work. Joshua barely eked out a living. Yet he was never hungry, had enough clothes to wear and had a roof, although small, over his head at night. Joshua was in fact a poor man, but he had pride and enough money to live on.

For Joshua, other than his work in metals, he loved books, all kinds of books. As he rarely had extra money for purchases beyond the basics needed for living, he would often stop by the public library to borrow books because it was free. He had done it for so long that the staff knew him well and grew to like the frequent visits and conversations.

One day while visiting the library the power went out. There was a side room where all the children's books were kept and the few kids present became frightened and started to cry. Joshua went to the truck, grabbed the menorah from its resting point and brought it into the building. He took some spare candles that the librarians had and went into the children's room. He lit the menorah. The kids circled around. Not quite knowing what to do, Joshua instinctively grabbed one of the books on the table and began to read.

The kids seemed fascinated. Joshua was a born storyteller. His face would contort to match the character he was reading about and his voice would follow. Spellbound the children listened. When it was completed they asked him to read another, to which he happily complied. At the conclusion of the second story the lights magically came back on. Joshua blew out the candles and returned to his truck.

A few days later Joshua paid another visit to the library. As he entered the building one of the children who were there the other day noticed him. She ran over and begged him to read another story. Joshua, quite embarrassed, was led by his hand back into the children's room. He picked up a book and began to read. Another child got up and asked Joshua to stop. Quite puzzled, Joshua asked why. The child said he wanted to see the shiny candlestick holder. Joshua got up, went out to the truck and brought in the menorah. The children once again gathered and listened intently while Joshua read them a story.

A routine developed. Every Friday afternoon, before sunset, Joshua would come to the library and read to the children, the menorah by his side. As word spread throughout the city, more and more children came with their parents. It was difficult to find a place to squeeze into the children's room.

The librarians did not seem to mind and liked the idea that the community was using the library. It also led to more people taking books out and a great reading program developed for the children.

One Friday afternoon Joshua did not show up. The kids crowded in but no one knew where he was. A call came from a nurse. Joshua was quite ill and although he wanted badly to come, he was confined to a bed in the hospital. Joshua had a nurse call the library to let them know, and he hoped he was not disappointing the kids.

The library staff went into the room and explained the situation. One of the parents stood up and said that he had an idea. A few of them should go to the hospital with a book and read it to Joshua. It might cheer him up. When the group tried to get in to see Joshua, the nurses said that there were too many people. A few of the kids asked if they could go in and the nurses said it would be fine. Joshua was surprised and when the kids started to read to him, a big broad smile came over his face.

Joshua, on one of his convalescent walks, noticed that a children's wing was but a few paces down the hall. Joshua hatched a plan. A few days later a few more kids and parents showed up at the hospital. He and a few of the visiting kids snuck into the children's wing. One of the parents, noticing Joshua's truck in the parking lot, went down, grabbed the menorah and set it next to him. Joshua began to read a story in the middle of a large ward of children.

At first when the nurses found out they were quite angry, but the smiles and calm faces of the children as they were being read to made a world of difference. Although against their rules, they did not have the heart to force Joshua to stop. Joshua went daily to the children's wing, with his menorah and a new book that the library had sent over.

Then one day a call came from the hospital to the library. Joshua had taken a turn for the worse and died during the night. On hearing the news, parents and children gravitated to the library in memorial for Joshua. His love of books, his concern for the community and his relationship to the children had meant so much too so many.

The library, as a lasting memorial to Joshua, brought in readers every Friday afternoon to read to the kids. They placed Joshua's menorah on top of a big case in the middle of the room for all to see. The hospital also created a type of memorial. They found that reading to the kids was a great benefit. They had an intern come in daily to read to the children. Someone had placed a small menorah in the room. The hospital decided to leave it there.

Word spread of what Joshua did and what the library and hospital were still doing. Other public facilities began to also set up rooms and times to read to the children. What was strange was that every time one of these rooms was created some type of menorah appeared. Sometimes it was a picture, sometimes an actual candleholder. It may have been big or small, real or a facsimile. Yet it was always present.

Midrash Tetzaveh
The Tallit

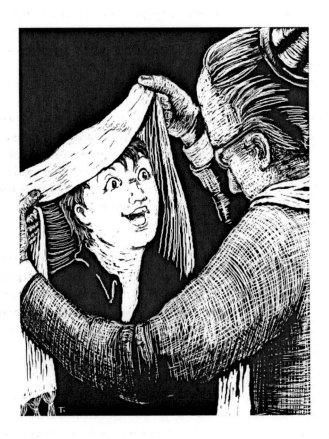

    Aaron had just turned twelve. It was one year until his Bar Mitzvah. Aaron started his lessons to learn the prayers and the part of the Torah he was to speak. The problem was that he could not find the excitement he thought he would feel and the learning proved very difficult.

Although a good student, he struggled through the simplest prayers and found no rhythm or structure with the torah portion he had to sing. As time went on, both he and his teacher grew worried that he was not progressing as he should. His tutor called his parents and explained that Aaron was not learning what he needed to, even though he seemed to be working at it. Aaron might not learn what he needs for his Bar Mitzvah.

Aaron's parents tried to help but it did not make any difference. They were also frustrated and worried. The whole thing was getting out of control. Aaron's parents lamented about the issue with Aaron's grandfather during their weekly phone conversation. His grandfather said he understood the problem and knew the solution. He would arrange to come for a visit and asked that Aaron's parents not say a word about this to Aaron.

Aaron's grandfather arrived a few days later with two large suitcases and an announcement that he would be visiting for a week. The following morning grandfather asked Aaron if he would go with him to the synagogue. He wanted to show him something. Aaron, who had a close relationship with his grandfather and liked spending time with him, agreed. Grandfather brought one of the large suitcases with him.

When they arrived, the rabbi let them in but then excused himself because of other duties. Aaron and his grandfather went into the sanctuary and up on the bimah (A raised platform in the sanctuary from where the service is led).

Aaron, his voice bordering on tears, told his grandfather of the trouble he was having learning the prayers and Torah portion. Aaron could not understand why it was so difficult for him. His grandfather said that he had made the trip to give Aaron an early Bar Mitzvah present. Aaron said he did not know if he could accept it as he did not know if he could go through with the Bar Mitzvah.

Grandfather smiled and walked over to the suitcase. He opened it and exposed a large garment within. Aaron could not yet tell what it was, although it filled the suitcase. As his grandfather lifted it out, Aaron recognized that it was a tallit, a prayer shawl. It was like no other prayer shawl he had seen except for one, the tallit his grandfather wore.

The shawl was huge! It was far taller than Aaron himself and even his tall grandfather had trouble lifting it out of the case. It was also beautiful. The color of the linen was copper, and reflected the light so perfectly as to make it seem like gold. The fringes were turquoise but a turquoise like he had never seen. This tallit created its own source of light and made the garment shine.

Grandfather asked if he could place the tallit over Aaron. Aaron exclaimed that it was too big to fit on his shoulders. Grandfather said, "Trust me!" He draped the tallit over Aaron's head. It covered him like a blanket. Not one speck of body poked from beneath the garment. For Aaron it was a strange experience. Light permeated the copper fabric creating a warm safe feeling.

Grandfather said, "I want you to feel the tallit. Let yourself be enveloped by it." The longer Aaron was surrounded by the tallit, the calmer he became, the easier he began to breathe, the further inside himself he was able to see. Aaron knew it wasn't magic but it was as if he could look at his very soul reflected against the inside of the garment. It did not scare him. It made him feel good, confident, and as alive as he ever felt.

Grandfather then asked Aaron to speak the prayer for placing the tallit on. As he spoke, the words rang out clear and loud. Grandfather asked if he could feel the kavanah- the heart of it? Aaron surprisingly said, "Yes". Grandfather then asked if he would say the prayers just before he would read for the Torah. Still under the tallit, he remembered the words and again spoke them loud and clear. "Did you feel the kavanah?" Aaron felt a smile emerge on his face and again said, "Yes"! The grandfather then folded over the large tallit and pinned it back over Aaron's shoulders in the same way that he wore his large tallit. They spoke the prayers again, together.

Aaron and his grandfather spent the rest of that day and in fact the rest of the week, going over his prayers and the Parasha, his biblical portion to be read on the day of his Bar Mitzvah. Every day, as they started, they each placed the tallit over their entire body and spent a few moments preparing to study. They then folded the linen back and pinned it against their shoulders. They studied the words and meanings together. The more Aaron understood about the prayers and the words of the Torah, the stronger, louder and clearer he sang. By the end of the week he had it down perfectly.

Aaron understood that it was not the tallit itself which allowed him to learn. Yet when he placed it on, his mind seemed to be able to focus in a way that allowed him to study, to question, and to pray. It allowed him to reach inside and live his religion with meaning, with feeling, with kavanah.

The day came for Aaron to recite from the Torah. The service began with a small ceremony when his grandfather formally presented the giant tallit to Aaron. Aaron, out of respect and love for his grandfather, gave him the first aliyah, the honor of saying the prayers just before reading from the Torah. And of course Aaron read the Torah perfectly.

Midrash Ki Tisa
The Golden Calf

The city was but a shell of a once strong proud community. Years ago people filled the streets, shopped in the neighborhood stores, worked in the teeming factories, and enjoyed the parks. But the factories moved, the shops closed and the parks deteriorated, leaving a scarred remnant of what once was.

The people reflected their city. Once proud, vivacious and energetic, they felt dispirited and enslaved. Memories of past success faded from their consciousness. They went to work daily, but it was mechanical and unfulfilling. A pall cast a long deep shadow over this city and engulfed all that it infected.

When despair achieved its low ebb, the city geared for an election for mayor. The political parties met and chose their respective candidates. The candidates met for a debate at one of the downtown parks. Not many residents showed up but the news reporters were there in force.

As the debate began, a group of teenage boys cornered a small child against a tree and began to poke and tease the child to tears. Although within earshot, the candidates continued their banter, ignoring what was going on adjacent to the stage. The press focused their cameras on the sideshow but did not bother to intervene.

The driver of a passing car, seeing the small child in tears, screeched his vehicle to a stop. A broad tall man exited the vehicle and swiftly moved toward the teen group, picking up a long tree branch that lay in the directed path. He parted the circle of teens with his staff, swooped in and picked up the child, placing the youth over his shoulder like a coddled baby lamb. The surprised teens escaped in all directions.

The man walked over to the crying mother and placed the child into her arms. The mother looked up and grasped the arm of the man. "Moses is that you?" she said. The man smiled, nodded, walked back to the car and drove off. The reporters surrounded the mother, ignoring the candidates, and began to ask questions. The mother remembered that the man was raised in this very city but had left as a young man. She could not quite remember why.

Within a few days, the reporters, already bored with the candidates, sought out Moses. They cornered him coming out of a market and asked him why he stopped to help the young child. Moses perplexed by the question responded, "Because he needed it!" and asked why none of the reporters tried to help the young child. The reporters ignored the query and continued with their own questions. Why had Moses returned to the city? Moses said that his mother, who still lived here, needed help with the very basics of life, like food and shelter. The company she worked her whole life for had gone out of business and took her retirement savings with it. The city would not help in the recovery of her savings nor with any other kind of assistance. He needed to make sure she was being taken care of.

The reporters spread out back to their respective organizations. The stories that they told said Moses, the savior of the young child at the park, blamed the government for the problems around the city. The candidates, felt angry that this outsider was receiving so much press, and challenged Moses to face them at that same park, to explain his views to the public. They never thought he would show, and felt they could receive that much more press from the event.

The day arrived and unlike the previous attempt, this event drew a multitude of the local citizens. The candidates again bellowed their rhetoric to any that would listen. As they were in mid form, Moses arrived. He moved through the crowd. The people spread before him, leaving a clear path to the stage. The candidates dissolved off the podium.

"Moses, Moses", the crowd chanted. Moses raised his arms to quiet the crowd. "There is a right. There is a wrong. You know the difference. Slavery is not only physical chains, but can just as easily be the way you feel inside. Cast off your chains and start to live." A man in the audience yelled that Moses should be mayor, that he could lead us out of this depression.

A groundswell of support carried Moses to an Election Day win. It was the only time in history that a person won as a write in candidate. Moses did not request that he be placed on the ballot and was reluctant to serve. After much prodding from the community, he accepted the job.

A few months later, Moses told the citizens he would go to Washington D.C. The entire country was having similar issues and the federal government had put together a program they thought might help the cities. Moses would go to review what they had and bring it back.

With Moses in Washington, the reporters riled up the citizens demanding action. They organized demonstrations which at times turned into riots. The council, trying to find a way through this uprising, turned toward anyone that could quell the turmoil.

A coalition of the political parties that lost the election suggested that the city build casinos. The tax money that they could levy as part of the gambling operations would raise enough to lift the city out of its depression. In a rush to judgment, the newspapers wrote that instead of waiting for new buildings to be constructed, they could set up a giant tent and begin operations immediately.

The council tried to get in touch with Moses, but he could not be disturbed. The federal offices had been sealed while the last of the plans were worked out. With the pressure mounting, the council approved the go ahead for a casino. A giant tent rose out of the very ashes of the city. Lights gleamed, gambling tables were erected and slot machines appeared as if by magic. Night and day the crowds teemed to the casino. It was a carnival atmosphere in the midst of the squalor of this city. A sign was placed at the entrance to the tent, "The Golden Calf".

The Federal Project was finally complete and Moses returned to the city. He brought a plan for new factories and jobs, sealed in a solid metal briefcase that had a covering that looked more like stone than steel. As he approached the city he noticed the tent, the lights... the casino. At first a very deep sadness welled up in his body. The sadness began to have a life of its own and turned to rage. By the time he entered the city, he lost control of his emotions. He took his car and smashed headlong into the casino sign.

Moses exited the car, and using the briefcase, smashed the pegs that held the tent up. The side walls folded onto themselves and collapsed into the adjacent mud holes. People fled in every direction. As Moses destroyed the last of the pegs, the briefcase itself broke into thousands of pieces.

His rage finally subsiding, the council approached. Moses berated them for their lack of backbone, their lack of faith. The council said that they could not communicate with Moses and simply tried to appease the citizens. The casino was to be a temporary solution, in case the Federal Government did not really have a plan.

The response was just too much for Moses. Tears streamed down his cheeks and his body went limp causing him to sit squarely on the ground. It was as if every ounce of strength left his body. The reporters slowly moved in, their cameras filming away. The crowd followed suit. Not a word was spoken, and no-one bothered to extend a hand to Moses.

As the crowd continued to tighten around the shriveled figure of a man, a small ripple distorted the encircling mass. A child broke through the crowd, stopped directly in front of Moses and grasped his hand. Moses recognized the child immediately. He rose from his sprawled position and hand in hand with the child walked through the mass. The people spread as if split by a knife. One by one, other children gravitated toward the two and together walked out of the park.

Midrash Vayakhel
The Pride of a Teacher

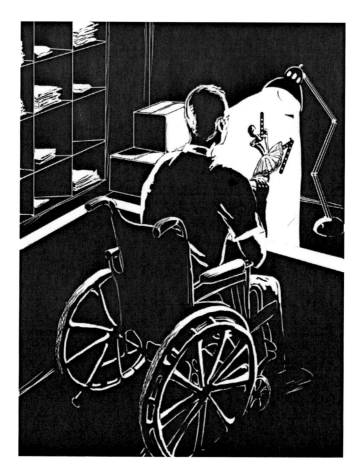

Arthur Bezalel worked as a clerk in the mail room of a large company downtown for years. He had suffered a wound in the war that left him paralyzed from the waist down and confined him to a wheelchair.

Life in the mail room wasn't exactly the stimulating work Arthur was looking for. Every day he diligently tended to his few simple tasks, trying his best to get them done quickly and effectively. When time allowed, he retired to a small, unnoticed corner to work on all manner of projects. He found that he could work with different materials, fabric, ceramics, even metal, and create unusual and beautiful objects of art. It was the part of his life that gave him happiness and fulfillment.

Things at the Company had been hectic ever since an electrical fire destroyed the top floor where all the top executives worked. Word had filtered down to the mail room that the Company was rebuilding the top floor to be the showcase of the city. Parquet wood floors, marble tables, the latest in communication technology and a multitude of extravagant purchases were made to accomplish the task.

"Arthur! Take this urgent overnight package to the top floor, and step on it!" Arthur's supervisor shouted at him from across the room. Arthur wheeled over, picked up the brown cardboard package, and headed into the elevator.

When Arthur reached the top, he saw workers moving back and forth around the floor. There were so many he couldn't even count them. It felt as if he had entered a human beehive. At the center of them all stood a large, portly man who argued ferociously with the construction team foreman. Arthur knew this man to be Marvin Middleton, the CEO of the Company and the receiving end of the package in his arms.

"A package for you, sir", Arthur said. Middleton grabbed the package, tore it open, and exposed a miniature version of the company's new logo. It was a complex piece of work that incorporated plastic, cloth, ceramics and metal in a three dimensional explosion of color. It had been designed by the most famous computer graphics group in the world. Middleton's mood turned ecstatic as he marveled at the emblem in front of him.

Mr. Middleton turned to the foreman and said, "I need this built at a scale 100 times this size and placed on the upper part of the glass window which opens on the city below." The foreman just shook his head, "We don't know how to do something that strange."

Arthur had an idea. "Um, sir?" he murmured. "I think I know how you could build this." The foreman glared at Arthur. "Now just give him a chance." Middleton told the foreman. "Continue young man." Arthur began to explain how the job could be done. "What is your name, young man?" Middleton asked. "Arthur, sir." He responded. "And what is it you do here?" Middleton inquired. "I work in the mail room, sir." Arthur said, pointing to the package. "Well, not anymore." Middleton said. "You work up here now. I'm convinced that you could do this job." Arthur shook his head. "Oh, no sir. I can't do this myself, I can't move out of this chair." he said. "No, no, boy!" Middleton chuckled. "I don't mean 'you' literally. You're going to teach these people here how to do what you were just talking about. They could learn a thing or two from a man like you."

Arthur thought about the idea of teaching others the skills that he had mastered in the dank mailroom below and it was an idea which pleasantly surprised him. He smiled and shook Middleton's hand agreeing to take on the task.

As the workers continued the rebuilding of the floor, the foreman provided a number of people to Arthur to build the logo. Arthur divided them into different groups based on the type material they were comfortable working with. He would explain a different technique to each individual based on the portion of the logo they were to work on. He did this sometimes by showing them small scale, in his lap while in the wheelchair. Other times he had some of the burly laborers pick him up and place him in a sling up in the air, to help them while working on the piece itself. From the street below, Arthur was seen through the large clear top story window and seemed to be suspended in mid-air, when in his sling. Slowly but surely, the variety of pieces came together into one masterful piece of work- the new Company logo.

The logo was revealed in a ceremony complete with the press and city dignitaries. As the tarp that hid the emblem came down, a photographer took a group picture of everyone who had worked on it. Someone counted the hundreds of people that Arthur had taught to bring this one project to a successful conclusion. In the middle of this crowd of engineers, architects, and construction workers sat a person in a wheelchair. There in the center, with the largest smile of anyone in the picture, a man named Arthur Bezalel, their teacher.

Midrash Pekudei
The Breastplate

There are some things in life that a person must have. For me it was a small breastplate like object. It was no more than about twelve inches square and had twelve different colored jewels embedded in a square array. It was awarded annually to the High School senior student who was deemed the smartest in the entire city. The twelve stones represented the twelve districts that made up the whole city.

Participants from across the metropolitan area competed for this prize. I could not jump high or run fast or out wrestle my baby sister, but I was smart. I set my eyes on the Breastplate when I was still in elementary school. Year after year passed, and I followed the competition keenly, always hoping to be the one to win that award when it was my time. Now as a senior, I would have my shot.

My father drove me to the competition. On our way out of the house, our neighbors came over to wish me luck. They had lived next door for as long as I could remember. They also had a son. He was severely mentally and physically handicapped. He attended a special school, and although nice enough, I really never spent any time getting to know him. His slow and unresponsive actions just frustrated me. I did not have the patience to deal with him. His name was Ariel, and he gave me a high five from his wheel chair on my way to the car, screeching a slurred set of tones that sounded like "good luck"!

The competition lasted all day. It combined a written with an oral examination. The written part began the competition. In this first segment, members of your own district were pitted against each other. Only the student with the highest score would be the one representing the district in the final phase. I scored the highest from our group, and now would face-off with the other district winners.

The second part involved the twelve district winners standing on a stage, being asked questions out loud. It was set up like a spelling bee. One competitor would be given a question. If that person got it wrong and another knew the answer, the first competitor was knocked out. The questions could be on any topic and were picked at random from a big rolling cage looking contraption.

The auditorium that held the final competition was large and packed with people. It had an aura of a sports arena, with parents and friends cheering their favorites, vendors selling their wares through the audience and a scoreboard showing both the person asking the questions, and the competitors. It was exciting and nerve wracking to be part of the spectacle.

One by one, my fellow participants were knocked out. I was able to answer my own questions and on occasion, one of theirs, to assist in removing other competitors from the stage. It was down to the last two contestants, me being one of them. My heart raced but my mind seemed calm and focused.

The question given to my opponent was a biblical one. What was the name of the person who was commissioned to build the Jewish tabernacle? My opponent did not know the answer. The question was given to me. I thought for a moment. I knew it was not Moses. Then I remembered an unusual aspect about the person. He was one of the only people in the bible that when named, had his genealogy not only go back to his father, which was customary, but also his grandfather. Then I remembered that there was a similarity between my grandfather's name and his. My grandfather was called Lale, but his friends always called him Busy Lale, because he was always on the go. Then I remembered. I answered loud and clear. The name of the person was Bezalel.

The crowd roared their approval. Confetti rained down from the rafters. Everything seemed to go in slow motion. The announcer made his way over and placed the Breastplate around my neck. It was the happiest moment in my life. My parents were so proud and I felt like I was king of the hill. There was a peacefulness about it. I could feel a smile go from one end of my face to the other.

For the next few days I felt like a celebrity. I wore the breastplate around school and everyone was patting me on my back and shaking my hand. From the students, to the faculty, to the people around the neighborhood, they all congratulated me. The warm fuzziness seemed to go on forever.

The citywide Special Olympics were going to be held at my High School. They asked if I would come and sit in the stands with the breastplate and support the program. I said I would be happy to. Toward the end of the day there was a wheelchair race halfway around the track. I noticed my neighbor Ariel was one of the participants. As they approached the starting line, I screamed his name and wished him luck. He raised his hand in recognition.

The race started and Ariel got off the mark pretty well. But as he went around the first turn, his limbs sort of went weak. Others began to pass and it was not long before he was dead last. The race continued and the other participants had finally crossed the finish line. People ran over to them and hugged and kissed them. Ariel was only about half way through and the more he tried the more he slowed down.

His parents finally came over and tried to push Ariel off the track. He screamed and got very mad. He was going to finish the race. After more time elapsed, the track officials said that they would have to remove Ariel, as the competition was over and they needed to close up the track. I came down from the stands and went to the side of a still slow moving Ariel. I took a loud speaker and asked that the crowd support Aaron until he finished the race. The crowd yelled in support and Ariel was allowed to go on. Yet he moved progressively slower and slower. After an hour, most of the crowd left. I remained at Ariel's side, imploring him on.

Another hour passed. There were only a few people left. Ariel, after what for him was a super human effort, finally crossed the finish line. When he did I yelled and screamed in delight. I danced around his wheelchair and threw confetti up in the air so that it would stream down over him. His parents sat in the adjacent bleacher their face's beaming with pride.

As it was close to dark I had my father bring his car around and shine his front lights on Ariel's wheelchair. I took the Breastplate from my neck and placed it around Ariel's. A smile went from one end of his face to the other.

A week later, Ariel's father came over to our house. In his hand was the Breastplate. He went to give it to me and I said that Ariel should keep it. He said Ariel passed away the night before and he wanted to return it. Tears well up in the father's eyes. He said that giving the Breastplate to Ariel made him so happy. It was the nicest thing anyone ever did for him. He thanked me and left. I hung the breastplate onto a spire off of the fireplace. I just could not seem to bring myself to place it back on. When I saw it, I could only think of Ariel. My father saw me struggle every time I looked at it.

A few days passed until it suddenly dawned on me what to do. I went to the sponsor of the breastplate competition. I asked their permission, which they gave. I then went to the Special Olympics office and asked if they would be so kind as to award the Breastplate to a person in their competition yearly that did not win their race but tried the hardest to finish. They liked the idea and agreed. The Breastplate would still go to the most deserving student in the city.

Midrash Vayikra
A Small Voice

Frank was content with his life. He was doing exactly what he wanted. He coached the High School's baseball team and for a second income worked as a vendor at the major league ballpark. Frank did not have much money, but he earned enough to support himself and was happy with what he was doing.

Frank's work style was unique. He had an operatic voice that he used often and loudly in both his chosen professions. When coaching baseball, he would teach his players the fine points of the game by raising his voice in clear, loud tones. His players would cower at the pointed tirade. They would not repeat their mistake, as they did not want that weapon pointed at them again.

At the ballpark, Frank would sell bags of peanuts in the stands. He used his voice to call out to the people in a particular section of the bleachers, with chants and rhymes, attracting their attention. He did not interrupt the game but did this between innings or long stoppages of play, which was often in the game of professional baseball. If the crowd liked what they heard, they bought out what bags he had in his possession. Frank would then go back into the concession area, refill his satchel with peanuts, and return to another bleacher section, repeating the act.

Frank worked these two jobs for years and used his magical voice to help him earn a living. One winter season he caught a bad case of the flu that turned into pneumonia. He was so sick he had to be hospitalized. During his sickness Frank would cough uncontrollably. The coughing scarred his vocal chords to the point he could no longer talk. The doctors tried to calm the coughing fits but could not do so. The scarring became permanent. Frank had lost his voice.

Frank, still lying in his hospital bed, became depressed. He had lost his most precious gift. The doctor walked Frank down to another wing of the hospital as part of his physical therapy. The doctor was called away on an emergency and left

Frank sitting in this unfamiliar area. The wing had a number of children in it but was also very different. At first he could not place it, and then suddenly it occurred to him. None of the children could speak.

Frank looked at these kids and noticed how much they interacted with each other. Many of them used sign language, others, physical gestures or facial expressions. They were communicating with each other.

Over the next few days, Frank returned to this area and slowly became involved with the kids. He started to learn sign language but more importantly, his attitude began to change. The children, even with their problems, always seemed to have a smile on their face, always seemed excited about something new or something coming up. Their enthusiasm was infectious. Although infections are not usually good in a hospital, this was just the medicine Frank needed.

Frank was finally released from the hospital. The school and ballpark did not think he would return to work, but Frank insisted he could find a way to do his job. The facilities decided to let him try. Over the next few months Frank worked out a plan.

Frank enlisted a few parents to help with the Baseball team, for when speaking was absolutely necessary. However, he found he worked with the players in a much more hands on manner. Instead of yelling instructions, he now moved to the position and demonstrated the proper technique. Frank found a simple pat on the back bolstered the confidence of a player. A high five for a play well done was far more effective in getting the player involved and enthused than yelling with his voice ever did. Frank found that his players would look for his facial expressions or gestures, and they worked far better as a team.

The vendor situation was more difficult to overcome. How could he attract customers in the stands if he could not use his voice? An idea came to Frank. He readjusted the shoulder straps of the satchel that contained the bags of peanuts in a way that freed up his hands. He took three bags out and began to juggle them as he went up or down the stairways. If people would call out to him to purchase a bag, Frank, in one deft motion, slung the bag in mid air to the customer. He then tapped the other two bags from mid air into his satchel, so he could await payment for the peanuts.

During timeouts in the game, Frank would demonstrate other juggling acts, such as doing four or five bags at one time or as groups of two. The crowd loved it. If the game was at a particular exciting moment, he simply stopped and slumped down so that the fans around could view the game without interruption. If the game was ongoing but slow, he might juggle only two bags, so as to not distract very much from the game. What Frank found was that he could now make sales at any time of the game. In the past, when he had used his voice, he could only make sales between innings. He sold more peanuts and made more money than he ever had before.

There were times when Frank missed his voice. He often remembered the sweet resonant tones he used to make. Yet now, he also understood how one could have a voice even without his vocal chords. And that small voice could be far more effective.

Midrash Tzav
Ritual

Rebecca's mother had a habit of placing her clothes on in the morning in a most unusual way. She laid out each article on the bed in a neat systematic manner. Her mother reached down very slowly, picked up one piece at a time and placed it on. She finished the act by smoothing the article out on her body. To end the ritual, she placed a hat on in a slow motion manner, cocked it to one side, placed her hands at her side, looked in the mirror, smiled and said, "Let's start the day!"

Rebecca, when very small, would mimic her mother when she dressed herself. Her mother caught her trying to imitate the ritual and decided from that time forward they would dress together. Both laid out their clothes on the bed next to each other, picked up the same article, in the same way, at the same time, and placed it on. They always finished by simultaneously placing a hat on their respective heads, moving their hands to their side, smiling and saying together, "Let's start the day!"

As the years rolled by, the ritual continued. Rebecca found that it not only cemented the bond to her mother, but left a positive frame of mind. It wasn't just a habit, but something that gave meaning and an optimistic approach to the start of the day.

When Rebecca was a teen, her mother passed away. It was a very sad time for her as she was close to her mother. She continued to place her clothes on in a ritualistic manner. It not only helped her prepare for the coming day, it was a way to honor and fondly remember her mother.

While in High School, Rebecca decided to find a job to make some spending money. There was an opening for some help at a Home for Abused Children. It was not a hard job, and the hours were flexible so as not to conflict with school. It did not pay much, but was enough to satisfy Rebecca's needs. She cleaned up around various areas, and helped the staff, as they needed it.

The wing of the building that she spent the most time in contained children who barely moved and would not speak. The doctors did not tell Rebecca much about these patients except that the early part of their lives was so bad as to cause them to revert inside themselves. Most of the other helpers hired by the Home did not want to work in this part of the building because it was so sad. Rebecca did not seem to mind and constantly talked to the kids as she did her various chores, even though they would not respond. The doctors liked her work and said if she would not mind spending all the time in this area, they would pay her more money without changing her number of hours. Rebecca agreed.

Over the next few months she continued to work in the "Quiet Wing", which was the nickname for this area. At the end of her shift Rebecca placed on a coat and hat in the slow manner that mimicked her morning ritual. She changed the final line of the act slightly to, "It sure is a nice day!" She noticed any number of children watching her put on her coat and hat. As she was about to leave one evening, one of the boys came near to her and moved as she moved, placed on a pretend coat and hat in a slow motion manner, and pretended to cock it to one side. Both placed her hands at their sides, looked in a mirror, smiled and said, "It sure is a nice day!" It was the first words this child spoke in five years. The doctors viewed the act from across the room and were shocked. Rebecca repeated the procedure the next day and not only did the child repeat the act and words, but others joined in.

The ritual seemed to make a connection with these children. Over time, because of this breakthrough, the doctors were able to work with these kids at a faster rate, helping them return to some kind of normalcy in their lives.

The newspapers and magazines caught wind of the story. They came out and interviewed the doctors and, of course, Rebecca. She became a star overnight. The public fell in love with the story and people all over the country imitated the ritual.

Rebecca was not overwhelmed by the attention. She enjoyed the experience and continued to work and go to school as she always did. Over time the publicity faded. The public eventually grew bored by the ritual and stopped doing it. The use of her technique did spread to similar hospitals which had the same success with their children.

Rebecca understood. The ritual had no meaning for the public. It was a habit with no substance, so it died. For the kids, the meaning of the ritual was different. It seemed to be a path for a return to a kinder, gentler world. For Rebecca, it was a connection to her mother and a way to start her day with a smile and a positive attitude. For any ritual to hold, it has to have meaning for those doing it. It was extraordinary that the meaning could be different for different people. Rebecca continued the ritual for the rest of her life.

Midrash Shemini
Middle America Kosher

Rob had a catering business in New York City. He specialized in banquets that required kosher foods. He knew many of the kosher butchers in town so he could supply the exact needs for a specific function.

The butchers he frequented constantly complained that they were finding it more difficult to get kosher meat. There were not enough kosher cattle processors and more were going out of business every year. Rob heard about one company going out of business next month in Iowa. He decided to make a visit to that facility.

He flew to Des Moines and rented a car to drive another one hundred and fifty miles to the small town where the facility was located. The owners of the plant gave him a tour. Rob was shocked. The plant processed meat all right, but it specialized in pigs. The owners were old and had decided to retire. Up to this point they could not find a buyer for the plant and if one was not found within the month they were going to demolish the facility.

Rob flew back to New York. He placed together a business plan that he thought might work. He set up a meeting of the New York City kosher butchers he knew. He explained the situation and proposed that they buy the plant as a group. They could clean it out and set it back up as a cattle processing plant that would supply their specific needs for kosher meat in the city. Rob would volunteer to move to Iowa to run the plant on their behalf.

The group liked the idea and formed a cooperative to purchase the plant. The offer to the facility owners was accepted. The following month the pig processing plant shut down and a large group of workers from New York showed up to clean and retrofit the facility. To say the least, there was culture shock in rural Iowa. The town was one hundred percent Christian. Most residents had never ventured out of this small village and the majority had never even met someone Jewish.

The townspeople, happy that the plant would survive and provide employment for the area, put together a welcome party for the clean-out crew and new owners. They closed off the main road, set up an area for bands and put out tables full of food. As the crew started down the street toward the party they suddenly stopped, turned around and went back to the plant. Rob concerned, went forward and looked across at the tables of food. He saw platters of pork ribs, ham, piles of pulled pork meat, ham sandwiches, and an entire pig on a spit.

The city council approached Rob visibly upset that their hospitality was so rudely dismissed. The city was famous for their pig products and put out the best that they had. Rob sat down with them and explained a little about kosher laws. Jewish people did not eat pig products of any sort. It was a forbidden food for these workers. The townspeople could not believe what they heard. They had never met anyone that did not eat pork. It was explained that the cleaned out plant would only handle beef, and even that would be restricted by certain guidelines for anyone working at the plant.

The incident created a real barrier between the New Yorkers and the townspeople. The crews felt that the residents set pork products out on the party tables to slight them; the residents thought that these foreigners from New York rejected their hospitality.

Rob knew that some bridge had to be built for the groups to get along. The plant would need the local residents to work there and since he, as well as other Jewish people, would be living in and around the area, some communication would be necessary. He went back to New York and met with the owner group. He explained the situation and asked for the group to donate some money to build a park for the local children. They agreed.

Over the next few months the clean-up proceeded and the park was under construction. Rob asked that all workers, both the Jewish New Yorkers and the local townspeople who were employed, to donate a small amount from their weekly checks into a charity fund for the town. A big Tzedakah Box was built by one of the workers and placed in a prominent location in the plant. Tzedakah is the Hebrew word for charity. The box was set up to collect contributions. Every week the employees added a part of their checks into the box. As the work was about to end, Rob took the money from the Tzedakah Box, and with it bought playground equipment which he placed in the new park. He invited the town to a grand opening of both the plant and the park.

This time the Jewish contingent brought the food. The townspeople were not sure they enjoyed the food, as some of it they had never heard of or tasted before. The New Yorkers stumbled around as well trying to learn how to square dance to the locally supplied music. The townspeople seemed very happy that a new park was in their community and the new playground equipment was a big hit with the children. The New Yorkers, although still not sure about the local residents, at least now knew that they could work side by side in friendship and respect. It was tough for anyone to stay mad at someone they danced with.

Over time the groups learned how to live together. There were still barriers between them, yet they now understood what was important to the other side and set up rules so as not to offend. For example, the plant shut down every Friday by 3 PM. This was so the Jewish side could go home and prepare for their Shabbat. As Sunday was the townspeople's Sabbath, the plant honored that by not reopening until Monday morning. The townspeople that worked at the plant learned all about kosher law and agreed not to bring any food into the plant. In return, the plant supplied meals to the employees when they worked.

Tensions still existed but the plant operated well and kosher meat was delivered on a regular basis to the butchers in New York City. As the townspeople learned a little more about Judaism, they adopted some of the mitzvot they liked. The workers asked that the Tzedakah Box remain as part of the plant. Everyone who worked at the facility, Jewish or not, contributed a percentage of their checks every week. The money was earmarked for some project within the community that could be enjoyed by all. A kosher plant in the middle of Christian America set an example for how different people can learn to live together in peace and mutual respect, without either having to lose their identity.

Midrash Tazria
The Malady

George decided at a young age that he wanted to become a doctor. He was smart, compassionate and loved the field of medicine. Early on in medical school he decided to specialize in Oncology. For the most part this involved the study of cancerous tumors, skin lesions and other physical ailments. George wanted to use his expertise as best he could to help the poor individuals who were unlucky enough to contract such maladies.

After graduation he contracted with a large city hospital to work in their Oncology Lab. He worked tirelessly on behalf of the patients, always looking for any way to help them. Unlike most other doctors in the lab, he would meet with the patients his lab work was responsible for. It did not help much in the mechanics of the lab work itself, but by placing a face with the paperwork, it prompted him to make sure his work was thorough and complete.

George sat down at his desk and reviewed the new files that were sent to the lab. One file in particular stood out. The doctors at the hospital seemed confused and could not properly diagnose the problem a particular patient had. They took a biopsy of lesions that covered this man's body and sent it to the Oncology Lab.

George ran a whole series of tests on the specimens. Everything pointed to a form of leprosy. Yet there was something very peculiar about the results. It was like leprosy but it was not leprosy from a medical point of view. George decided to visit the patient.

As George entered the room he could see the patient lying on top of the bed, most of his body exposed. He was covered from head to toes in blister-like sores. George looked at his chart. His blood pressure, temperature and all other vital signs were perfect. The hospital took samples of blood and from the blisters, looking for a virus or any clue as to the cause of the physical ailment. There were no signs of any abnormality that would cause these sores.

George talked with the patient. His name was
Naaman, an unusual name originating from his parent's
ancestral land. He worked for a large city newspaper and had
recently received a promotion to head the Editorial
Department. Naaman was married and had three children.
Life seemed to be very positive for Naaman, except he had
these sores that no-one could diagnose.

Medically there was nothing that pointed to a cause of
the disease. The journals George scoured said sometimes
physical issues can be caused by mental problems and
therefore physical tests would not help in a diagnosis. George
decided to investigate more about Naaman outside the Lab.

A few weeks of digging came up with a most interesting
sketch of this patient. Yes, he was recently promoted to a very
important position at the newspaper. Yet to get the position he
undermined his competition at the office through the use of
gossip and taking credit for the work of others. Yes, he had a
typical family, but he spent no time at home and was not
involved in his children's life in the least. What seemed like a
very nice stable life on the outside was in fact a disaster at the
foundational levels.

George visited Naaman in his room. Naaman was
depressed. He had been isolated and alone for many days, as
the doctors did not know if what he had was contagious and
took precautions by not allowing visitors. George and Naaman
talked for some time. Naaman understood the reality of his
life. The time alone made him reflect on his actions. Naaman
wanted to try to correct the situation. He felt he would never
leave this room again and needed to make peace with those he
wronged.

George arranged for Naaman to have the communication tools he needed. He placed a phone, a fax, and a computer to write letters, in his room. Over the next week Naaman worked to fix the reputations of those he hurt and to ask forgiveness from his associates and families. Although he could never totally repair the damage he caused, he at least mitigated the effects.

As the week progressed the lesions on his body began to reduce. The first sign was the disappearance of the blisters from his face and scalp. The ones on his body reduced in size but remained. The nursing staff came in daily and meticulously washed Naaman's body. His hospital garment from the day before was burned and he was given a new one to wear that day. George visited Naaman daily just for them to talk. It seemed to lift Naaman's spirits and gave him more resolve as to the actions he wanted to take the following day.

Naaman lost his job at the newspaper when they learned of his past actions. He understood why they let him go and accepted the consequences. His wife and children were leery at first. They did not know if Naaman was sincere, but visited him daily for a short period of time. They could not go into the room but talked across a glass window and intercom. Over the next few weeks they slowly began to trust Naaman and new strong bonds began to grow.

Over the next month the lesions disappeared. The hospital staff still did not have a clue as to the cause of the sores. George, although he could not prove it, felt that the physical problem was a result of Naaman's actions and that Naaman himself could not condone what he did. Just before Naaman's release from the hospital they talked again.

George told him what he thought caused the sores. Naaman agreed. He knew that the other doctors could not find a reason for the malady. He also knew that when he truly understood that his actions were wrong and acted to correct it, that the sores began to disappear. Even if the other doctors did not believe, Naaman did. And his actions for the rest of his life would never be the same.

Parasha Metzora
A Reflection from Within

    Richard was the star actor of the local theater company.
When he performed all eyes were riveted on him. Other
actors who happened to be on the stage at the same time
melted into the background. As talented as he was, he was also
self absorbed, conceited and brash to any other person in his
vicinity.

Richard always searched for new ways to keep the center of attention. He wanted to be the best and wanted everyone around him to know he was the best. The theater company was to do a version of *Dr. Jekyll and Mr. Hyde.* Although very good during rehearsals, Richard sought for something extra. His Mr. Hyde just seemed to be missing something.

After one of the rehearsals, a knock came on the Richard's dressing room door. One of the new bit actors at the theater entered. The actor said he knew that Richard was looking for an edge to play Hyde and he had just the thing for him.

Richard at first dismissed him but as the man turned to leave the room, he had second thoughts. "What kind of edge can you provide?" The man said he befriended an actor in London who gave him a potion. The Londoner said it was very powerful and would create a skin disorder that would reveal itself when he turned into Hyde.

Richard said that it was fantasy and to stop playing games. The bit actor said, "The biggest problem with the potion was that it reflected the inside of a person. It would only work on actors who had a mean soul. I have seen you act and feel it would work just fine."

Richard, insulted, asked him to leave. The man turned to exit the dressing room but laid the bottle of potion on the dresser. "You must remember to only take a little and know that the effects may last up to a week." Richard again asked the man to leave and said he did not believe in such witchcraft. The man exited, leaving the bottle.

The theater company put on their first performance of the play. It had gone fine but was not the typical blockbuster that the audience grew to expect. Richard felt desperate. He would only accept the best and his desire for the audience to love him and his performances was overwhelming.

As Richard was about to leave his dressing room for the start of the next performance, he glanced at the bottle sitting on the table. He was going to dismiss it again when his drive for a top performance stopped him in his tracks. Without a second thought, Richard grabbed the bottle and drank the contents.

The performance was going well but still was not living up to expectations. As they approached the finale, and Richard did his final transformation into Hyde, he noticed something strange began to happen to his skin. Within seconds his now hunched body was covered with leprous sores. The ugliness seemed magnified in the stage spotlight. The audience gasped in terror.

Richard finished the show and the audience gave him a standing ovation. Still covered in sores for the curtain call, the audience roared their approval, thinking Richard's look was the result of a master makeup artist. The cast and director were stunned and did not quite know what to do or think. Ultimately they dismissed it as just another attempt by Richard to upstage everyone else.

Richard returned to his dressing room and locked the door behind. He tried to wash the sores off his body, to no avail. The Londoner knocked on the door and stuck his head inside. He told Richard, "The minute I saw what happened on stage I knew you drank the potion." He said, "You must be very mean on the inside to have so many prominent sores. He had never seen such a reaction to the potion before." He reminded him that it would be a week before it wore off. "However, as mean as you are, it just might be permanent."

The performance was the last of the weekend. Richard would have five days before the next scheduled show. He was sure to find a cure by then. Richard finished dressing and slung a large cape over his body. Coupled with a large hat, he was covered so that no-one could see him, and left for home.

A few days passed but the sores got no better. If Richard went to a hospital he most likely would miss a performance, which he never did. He was also afraid that they would put him away if they could not find out what it was that had infected his body. Richard decided he would not leave his room.

By the fifth day, Richard was getting stir crazy. He needed to get out. Yet the sores persisted. He decided he would go out covering his body with the same cape he used when leaving the theater. He walked to a nearby park. The sun was out and it was quite warm. He sat on a bench near a children's playground.

Suddenly, a child lifted the cape to see what was underneath. Richard did not see the child, as the cape had the same effect of hiding his vision from everyone else as well as it hid their sight from him. Exposing the hideous sores, the child screamed. Richard jumped at the frightful sound and the cape fell to the ground revealing the rest of his body. The sight of the hideous sores caused the children and parents to scream in terror.

Richard fled the park as fast as his legs would carry him and returned to the apartment. Looking at the mirror, he saw sweat running into the sores covering his head. It was no better on his arms or legs. The Londoner said that the potion reflects only what was on the inside. How could his inside be so ugly? Richard feared that the sores would never go away. He may never be able to act again. The thought sent a bolt of fear, trepidation and outright anguish through his wracked body.

Richard called the theater and said that he was too ill to perform. He would let them know when he could return. For the first time in his life, Richard felt like he was lost. And the loneliness was almost too much to bear. He knew he was not nice to others but he loved the theater. He was rude to other actors but that was because he thought they would try and upstage him. If the sores did not go away, he would lose the one thing that he loved most in life- the theater. He may never hear the roar of an audience and he would even miss the interplay between his fellow actors.

Richard closed all the blinds to the windows of the apartment and kept it pitch black inside. Even he did not like to look at the physical deformities. The week passed. Getting up, Richard moved to a mirror in the dark room. He feared that when he turned on the light, the sores would still be there. He braced himself for the moment of truth. Is the ugliness inside so great that the sores would never leave?

Flipping on the light exposed a clear, bright, smooth, soreless face. Richard examined his arms, then his legs. No sores. Turning on all the lights, no trace of the leprosy was found. In almost paranoia fashion, he stripped the sheets off his bed and placed them and all his clothes in a washing machine. He must have washed them five times to make sure no trace of the contamination would be left. Richard bathed himself all afternoon. He washed every crevice, every hair and every molecule of his body. He made sure none of the contamination would be left.

Richard returned to the theater. He still strived for the best performances he could possibly squeeze out. Yet his approach toward others changed. He was mindful of the other actors, cordial to strangers and far more attentive to those around him. The other actors saw the change. It was not an extreme change but a change nonetheless. Richard had become a mensch, a real human being, a person that others could look up to. He still wanted perfection but it sprang from a foundation of goodness. Richard went on to have a remarkable successful career. He had but one major problem at the theater: He would never play *Dr. Jekyll and Mr. Hyde* again.

Midrash Acharei
To Be a Jew

Jonathan, Alan and Irwin were the best of friends. They had known each other for as long as they could remember. Their birthdays were but one week apart and they always celebrated together. Last month, when they turned twelve, they got box seats for a baseball game right behind the dugout of the home team.

The boys all lived in the same neighborhood, went to the same school, and had the same interests. They would talk about classes at school, girls and just about most any topic. But the real common bond was sports. They would watch or play whatever professional sport was active at that moment.

It was mid-September and the main order of interest was football and the baseball playoffs. For Jonathan it also marked a time he did not particularly enjoy. It was the Jewish High Holiday season. Yom Kippur was that Sunday and his family would spend the entire day at the synagogue. Alan and Irwin were not Jewish and teased Jonathan about missing the games on television. They would be thinking of Jonathan as they enjoyed watching all the games.

On Saturday, the boys decided to go the school and play some basketball on the outdoor courts, as the weather was so nice. They were taking a break on the side of the court when Alan noticed one of their classmate's crossing over the field. Irwin said his name was Ben, and he was considered a nerd at school. He was one of those kids that never played sports and, to the best of his knowledge, had no friends.

The boys decided to have some fun at Ben's expense. As Ben crossed the court, Irwin rolled the basketball hard against Ben's feet. Ben, not seeing it coming, tripped and fell against the hard concrete. The CD player he had been carrying flew out of his hand and crashed against the court, smashing into pieces. The boys rolled over with laughter. Jonathan walked over to the sprawled out Ben and slipped the earphones off his head. He flipped them to Alan who dropped them on the ground, squished them under his foot, and exclaimed in a whimsical manner, "Oops!"

Ben slowly got up from the ground. He brushed himself off, straightened his eyeglasses and nearly in tears, walked off without saying a word. The boys seeing this spectacle roared again with laughter and returned to playing basketball.

The next morning Jonathan got ready for synagogue. He vowed to fast this year. He would be a Bar Mitzvah the following year, and fasting on Yom Kippur when he reached that age forward would be required. This year he could practice to make sure he could do it. Normally, Jonathan was bored by the services. His mind would wander to anywhere else but where he was. He would think about the games he was missing on television or even school; anything not to listen to the service.

Jonathan did not know if it was the lack of food or simply being another year older, but he actually began to listen to the prayers. There was one prayer that stood out. It was said a number of times. It went something like, "for sins against God you have to ask God for forgiveness, for sins against another human being you have to ask forgiveness from that person, not God".

Jonathan's thoughts kept going back to Ben. Although it seemed funny at the time, the more he thought about what they did, the more it bothered him. After services he went to visit Alan. He told him that he was upset about what they had done to Ben. Jonathan asked if it also bothered him. Alan said it did, but he took care of it. Jonathan asked how. Alan said that when his family went to church that morning he confessed to what they did. The priest said if he was truly sorry for what he did, and would say a certain numbers of prayers, that God would forgive him. Alan said the prayers and now felt much better.

Jonathan then went to see Irwin. He asked if he felt bad about what had happened. Irwin said not at all. It was survival of the fittest and they were showing Ben who was the better man. Irwin told Jonathan that he needed to look out after himself and not worry about others. That was how to get ahead in life.

Jonathan did not understand. Alan in no way helped or apologized to Ben, and Irwin did not even care. Jonathan remembered the prayer from the synagogue and decided to act. He went to the store and bought a new CD player and earphones. He went to Ben's house and asked to see him. He told Ben he was sorry for what they did, gave him the replacement equipment and asked if he would be so good as to forgive him.

Ben, at first leery about the present, looked it over. It was actually a better player than the one he had. He asked if Jonathan would like to come in. For the next few hours the boys talked. It was true that Ben did not like sports, but he did like music and computers. Ben showed Jonathan the latest computer game and they played it on a wide screen television in Ben's basement. The two talked and played for hours.

Over the next few months Jonathan continued to play sports with his old friends, but now also spent time with Ben. Whole new worlds opened up to him that he never knew existed and truly enjoyed. He noticed other people, other places and some pretty neat things right within his own neighborhood. Before, the world extended no further than how far Jonathan's own arm reached. Now he saw much more. He began to understand the word, community.

The next year, Jonathan looked forward to attending Yom Kippur services. When the prayer was said about asking forgiveness, it held a most special meaning. He noticed many of the prayers that day were as much for the group, as it was for the individual. The word community took on yet another level of meaning.

Jonathan felt for the first time a sense of what it meant to be Jewish. When it came to relationships with other people, he did not understand Alan, and he really did not understand Irwin. They were still friends, but they had different beliefs.

Jonathan felt comfortable with his beliefs. It was like buying a new coat. You try one on and it just does not feel right. You try on another and it feels like it was made for you. Judaism seemed tailored made for Jonathan. It just felt right. It felt good to be Jewish.

Midrash Kedoshim
The Kohen Gadol

     Aaron was to be a Bar Mitzvah in a few short months. Relatives were coming in from out of town and many friends were going to attend the day he was to recite from the Torah. Yet he just could not get excited about the event. In fact, it held no meaning for him whatsoever.

Aaron studied with a tutor one time per week, but was not making any progress in what he needed to learn. He was having trouble even speaking the Biblical lines, let alone singing them and the translations or meanings were not even remotely possible. His Biblical portion came from Parasha Kedoshim. He knew it was about the priests taking over the operation of the tabernacle but that was the extent of it.

Aaron was interested in just about anything but his Bar Mitzvah. This particular week he did not even bother to go to his tutoring lesson and spent the time playing baseball with his friends. His parents were quite angry with him but he just did not seem to care.

That evening, when Aaron fell asleep, he had a most peculiar dream. When he woke his body shook uncontrollably. Aaron strained to remember some of the details of the dream. He remembered seeing a flash of lightning. It was as if he was behind a camera. The scene slowly came into focus. It was a desert setting.

The camera panned closer and the setting became clearer. There was a small raised platform that had a tent like structure in the center. Two people stood at the entrance to the tent. The first held a staff in his hand and had a long flowing white beard. It was Moses. He was very angry and berating the second person. There was a huge crowd of people surrounding the tent. The second person ignored Moses and did not pay attention to the crowd.

The camera turned from Moses toward the second person. It focused at first on a breastplate and ceremonial robes. It was the High Priest. As the camera moved up to see the face of the High Priest, Aaron strained to remember what he could about him. A tremor came over his body as he remembered that the name of the Priest and his own was the same. The face of the High Priest came into focus and it was Aaron himself. The High Priest turned toward the people. He saw them slowly sink into the sand, calling out his name, outstretched arms pleading to him, eventually disappearing from sight. This is when Aaron woke, his body shaking all over.

Aaron dismissed the nightmare and thought it must have been caused from some bad food he ate earlier that day. Ominously, each night the nightmare returned. It was always the same, yet always a little different. Wherever his gaze went at the end of the dream, that item disappeared into the sand. One night it was Moses, another night it was the Torah Scrolls, and another the tabernacle itself. He always heard the pleadings of the people ringing in his ears and those pleadings were always directed to him, Aaron, the High Priest.

On every night for the next two weeks the nightmares came. Every night Aaron woke, shaking, in a cold sweat, scared. He had to find a way to make them stop. He thought he might find the answer in his Torah reading, as it was about the High Priest. He read the translation that his tutor gave him but it provided no clues, and the nightmares continued.

Aaron, still thinking it had something to do with his Torah portion, went to the library to find what other people said about this Biblical portion. He found many books that tried to explain the meaning behind the words. The Parasha listed different mitzvoth, good deeds, that the priests were to follow. One phrase stood out. "You shall observe all My decrees and all My ordinances, and you shall perform them." Aaron did not understand why the last part of the sentence was needed. If a person observes the mitzvot, is that not enough?

That night the nightmare changed again. It began the same way but after panning to the breastplate and robes, a second flash of lightning filled the sky. Aaron looked up and saw words written against the sky. It said "and you shall perform them". He woke, yet did not feel the cold sweat or the tremor but visualized the words written in the sky. Then it dawned on him. There are many negative mitzvot, all the ones that start "Do Not", such as "Do Not Kill". A person can observe these by simply doing nothing at all. The phrase at the end of the Parasha sentence is added because a person must also do positive acts. There must be action toward or with other people; you must *perform* them for Judaism to have meaning.

That night there was no nightmare. There was a dream. This time Moses was not berating Aaron, but standing with him, smiling, facing the people. The people were not screaming for help, but praying together and singing songs. There was no thunderstorm, but a shining bright sun. And when the sand shook, the people did not sink but trees and flowery bushes sprung up among the people.

Over the next few months Aaron set aside time to work in the community. He donated time to a local shelter, helped tutor small children at the school and even did various chores around the house. The day came when Aaron recited the words of the Torah in front of the congregation. In the course of trying to find the meaning behind the words, he consequently learned the Hebrew perfectly. And the words he spoke that day held a special meaning for him, as did the Judaism he now understood in a new light. The nightmares never returned.

Midrash Emor
Celebration of a Holiday

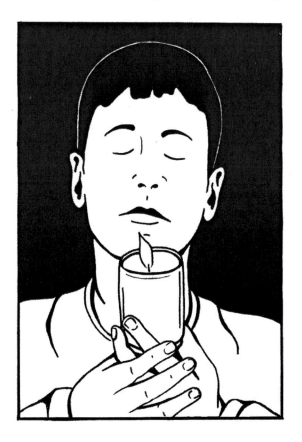

Jason was celebrating his twelfth birthday. It was a quiet kind of party. His mother made his favorite foods for dinner, and together, with his grandfather, they ate the meal without much conversation. Afterwards he opened a few presents and thanked all for their thoughts.

Jason's family was comfortable. His father made a nice living as a manager for a big company. They lived in a nice house and he never remembered wanting for much of anything. Jason was an only child and his grandfather lived with them. He can't remember his grandmother as she died when he was about three years old. That was when his grandfather moved into the house.

His grandfather was about the strangest person Jason had ever known. He barely spoke a word to anyone. Retired, he would spend his time fiddling with broken tools or meandering around the house doing this or that, but nothing in particular. His grandfather had been a Holocaust survivor. His first wife and his own parents died when the Nazis invaded Poland. He spent the war in a concentration camp. He never spoke of that time, not even to Jason's father, his son.

When Jason was little, he noticed a number tattooed on his grandfathers arm. He tried to ask him about it and all his grandfather did was cover it with his hand and slowly walk out of the house. His mother, overhearing the question, warned Jason never to ask his grandfather about the tattoo. It hurt him too much to talk about it. When Jason was ten his father told him about his grandfather and explained what the Holocaust was.

A survivor from the same concentration camp came over one day. As was typical, Jason's grandfather walked out of the house without saying a word. The other survivor had a picture taken by soldiers who liberated the camp. In the middle of the group photo was his grandfather. An ashen sack of skin and bones, Jason barely recognized his grandfather.

His eyes were sunk back into his head and his skin was loosely draped over brittle visible ribs. He could not have weighed more than 70 or 80 pounds. The other survivor said that his grandfather stopped speaking when the Germans killed his family in front of his eyes.

After the war his grandfather went to America, eventually remarried and had one child, Jason's father. His grandfather worked hard to support his family but even after all those years, his grandfather would only utter the fewest of words and then only if absolutely necessary. As Jason grew he would often peer into his grandfather's face. It was very wrinkled but had a strange plumpness about it. His eyes...his eyes were deep black and if you looked real hard at them you could get lost in all that darkness.

Although the family was Jewish, Jason did not remember doing anything religious. They never went to a synagogue or had any sign in the house that would show religion. His family knew they were Jewish, and it was a perfectly acceptable label which the family held in high regard.

One spring day, as Jason walked down the street, a classmate noticed him in front of her house and invited him in. She said that it was Passover, that it was their custom to invite others to their celebration and asked Jason if he would like to join them for dinner. Without thinking much he entered the house.

Everywhere he looked he saw tables filled with food, filled with wine, filled with people. The next four hours seemed a blur. Stories, blessings, and most of all song filled the house. It was like a balloon you keep pumping air into, waiting for it to burst at any second. The joy was overwhelming. His ears rung with the volume of talk that enveloped the room and Jason found himself trying to join into the songs. His heart raced with excitement. It was a beat he never felt before. He thanked his friend and her family at the end of the evening and went home.

A few days later he saw his classmate at school, again thanked her and exclaimed, "He had never had such a great time before." She said, "If he wanted he could join them for a Shabbat dinner and stay with them as they went for services to the synagogue." He confessed, "Although he was Jewish he had never been to the synagogue and would feel out of place." She said, "Don't worry! Her family would be happy if he went with them."

Jason had to and wanted to accept the invitation after the experience of the Passover celebration. He felt excited but nervous, as he did not know what to expect. A few aunts, uncles and cousins of his friend had joined for the Shabbat meal. Her mother lit candles, her father said a few prayers, they drank a glass of wine, and everyone took a piece from the large Challah bread centered on the table before dinner was served. The food flowed from the kitchen and was warm and inviting. Like Passover, the conversation was never-ending. The noise was so different from what he was used to. His house was quiet, reserved. In this house a knife could be used to cut the words thick in the air.

After supper a few more prayers were chanted and then everything stopped. Not a clang of glass or silverware, not even the sound of people breathing. Then slowly, almost in a whisper, her father began to sing a few notes of a Hebrew song. Her mother joined harmonically. In turn, others around the table entered the song. As more joined in, the song got a little faster, a little louder. As the final cousins entered the fray, a few of the uncles jumped up and began to dance around the table- joined together via an overhead napkin. As they circled the table, others stood and joined the line. The joy and warmness of Passover was just as apparent this Shabbat eve. He asked his classmate, "Is this a special Shabbat", and she responded saying, "No, it was like this every Friday night."

Over the year Jason joined his friend's family for many Jewish celebrations. He attended services often and they were very much like the home celebrations- prayer, conversation and plenty of song. How Jason loved the songs. The rabbi told Jason that there was a synagogue in Jerusalem that did the entire service in song. The congregation sat in a large circle and harmonized the entire service. Jason vowed one day to travel to Israel to see such a service.

His friend had invited Jason's family on a number of occasions to join them for one of the holidays but they would not. Jason tried to get his family to celebrate a Shabbat at their home but it was such a foreign concept that it failed miserably. It was not that they did not understand what Jason was trying to do but it was not in their nature.

156

As the years passed, Jason found himself continually drawn to a Judaism that celebrated life. He enjoyed the way it made him smile and feel part of the community. Jason understood how Judaism for his grandfather was just as important but different. The Holocaust had driven his religion deep within. It was so deep that words could not escape. Jason knew that if he had to face what his grandfather did, he might not be strong enough to survive. Judaism certainly shaped them both but how so differently.

Jason's grandfather passed away late that summer. There was no real funeral. Jason and his parents went to the cemetery and watched his grandfather lowered into the ground. The gravestone did have a Jewish star and mentioned both his parents and Jason. Like his grandfather's life, no words were uttered that day.

That Friday night Jason attended services at the synagogue. The rabbi, who had taken a special interest in Jason, had gone over to console him. Jason asked if it was proper to recite the prayers of mourning for his grandfather, as he knew his parents would not and did not think his grandfather would approve. The rabbi said he understood. "Jason, Jewish prayers are for the living, and as it is your way to pray, it is not only acceptable but proper. Your grandfather gave for his family, for his people, in his way, and that is something well worth remembering and giving honor to."

Jason would remember his grandfather every year, on the anniversary of his death. He would light a candle, say a prayer and sing. For it was the way Jason celebrated not only the holidays but life.

Midrash Behar
A Sabbatical Year

Aaron worked on a large farm in Texas. The farm had a most unique benefit program for its employees. After working for six years on the farm, the workers received the seventh year off with pay. The program created loyalty to the company and hard working employees. Aaron was about to finish his sixth year when he thought of how he might spend that year off.

Aaron decided to spend the year visiting Israel. He wanted to live in Jerusalem and learn as much as he could about his Jewish heritage. He contracted with a housing development that rented him an apartment for the year and made his final travel plans.

Aaron arrived at the Tel Aviv airport. He stepped down the stairs from the airplane to the tarmac. Just setting his feet on the ground sent shivers down his spine. He did not consider himself a very religious person, yet he felt comfortable, at home, just walking on this land.

Aaron arrived in Jerusalem and quickly settled into his apartment. The Old City of Jerusalem could be seen from the back porch. It was on the top of a mountain and loomed tall and majestic. He decided he would wait six days, and on the seventh would venture within its gates. For those first days he explored the surrounding streets, always with an eye toward the Old City. The wait proved exciting and unbearable. The anticipation grew with each passing day.

The seventh day arrived. He rose early out of bed, ate a quick breakfast and began to walk toward the entrance gate a few miles away. The closer got, the larger the view became. He felt his heart race as he climbed the last stretch of mountain to the gate.

Inside the walls, the old city teemed with people. The streets moved around him in a maze and were filled with nooks and crannies. Shops filled both sides of the streets and traveling down the cobblestone paths was difficult. Yet there was something different and vibrant compared with the rest of Jerusalem.

After a few hours of wandering, Aaron decided to stop for some refreshment. Without knowing it, he had wandered into the Arab quarter of the city. He had read much about the Israeli-Palestinian conflict but had not really paid attention. After drinking a cup of strong coffee he stood to leave. Suddenly he felt a heavy bang on his head and blacked out.

The next thing Aaron knew he was being held by an odd looking old woman. It was dark all around. He was in some sort of back alley lying in a puddle. Putting his hand to his head he felt blood dripping off his matted hair; then Aaron blacked out again.

Aaron awoke on a bed, in a room he did not recognize. The room was small with thick white walls. His hand moved up around his head, feeling a bandage wrapped around his skull. He was weak and could barely move. Aaron noticed his clothes piled neatly in the corner. He was in a white caftan-like robe.

Aaron recognized the old lady from the alley as she entered the room. She jabbered on endlessly. He could not understand what she said because she spoke Hebrew and he did not know the language. He had memorized a few prayers in his youth and could recognize the language, but that was the extent of it. Then, a younger person entered and he introduced himself in English. His name was Ari.

Aaron learned from Ari that he had entered the wrong part of the Old City. Tensions were high and Americans were not welcomed by the Arab population in that area. Aaron was hit over his head and dumped in an area outside the Arab quarter. He did not see the person who did it or in any way comprehended why.

Ari's grandmother found Aaron in the alley. She and others helped him back to their house. A doctor came and fixed him up, although he said that Aaron should not move for a few days because of a concussion. Aaron understood and slumped back down to sleep.

After a few days, Aaron began to feel better. The doctor came by daily to check him over and change the bandages. The grandmother, forever chattering away, entered the room three times a day to bring him food. He finally rose from his bed to look around.

Aaron was amazed. There were but two rooms in the house, the bedroom and a family room. The people that found him and helped him were poor; yet they gave him their only bedroom and fed him food they probably needed themselves. The neighborhood around them was not much better. As Aaron continued to convalesce at the front doorway the local residents would stop by, talk and bring their greetings. It was always with a smiling face, a warm handshake and a spry "Shalom"! The people may have been poor but they were optimistic and friendly.

A week later, Aaron was finally able to return to his apartment. He really did not want to leave the Old City. He enlisted the help of the grandson and a few of his friends. The group entered a local market. They bought lots of food and had a party for everyone on the Old City block. It was Aaron's way of saying thank you.

The day after the party, he again went shopping, but this time for furniture and tools and other household items to help the family and their neighbors on the block. Aaron spent the rest of his Sabbatical year, in this neighborhood, building, repairing and teaching others skills that he had learned when growing up. Aaron started to learn a little Hebrew. He felt more at home and more Jewish than he had ever felt before.

The year ended and it was time for Aaron to go home. He felt bad about leaving his new friends and they would certainly miss him, but everyone knew it was time to go. He thanked the family again for helping him when he was hurt and bid all a fond Shalom.

Aaron returned to Texas. He was happy to be back, but at the same time missed his other home in Jerusalem. He went to town to stock up on groceries and other items. Coming out of the store he looked around at the city.

He never noticed the local community before, as his thoughts always centered on the farm. He saw a food shelter down the block. He dropped the groceries into the car and went to the shelter. He peered inside and saw people lined up for food; people that were really in need. He walked up to the manager of the shelter and asked if he could help. The manager said they were about to run out of food and did not know what to do. Aaron grabbed a few of the residents, went back to the grocery store and bought everything he could lay his hands on. They went back to the shelter and passed out the food.

Aaron returned to work, but over the next few weeks he spent time helping out at the shelter. He also joined other local charitable organizations. Aaron had changed. He understood that charity was not something restricted to Israel. It had to be done wherever it was called for, and most especially in his own local community. It was a connection to the land, whether it was the farm or Jerusalem itself. It was a connection to community, whether it was on the other side of the globe, or right there in his small Texas town. To help another person when in need was perhaps the most Jewish thing Aaron could ever do. He had found his heritage.

Midrash Bechukothai
A Valuation

David owned a small grocery store in the middle of the neighborhood. What set his small store apart was that he personally inspected and bought all the items that were placed in the market. He went to the terminals where the produce and other foodstuffs were brought in to the wholesalers at the unreasonable hour of 4 am. After picking out only the best produce, for the best price he could find, it was loaded onto his truck and transported to his store.

When the food was unloaded and placed on the shelves, he would go bin to bin, pricing each item based on the valuation he calculated from the early morning purchases. It was the time that David liked best. He had a knack for numbers and for understanding what went into the ultimate price of an object.

Numbers were David's forte. He thought that if he wasn't a grocer, he probably would have been an accountant, although he did not like to sit behind a desk. On occasion, David hired extra help. He calculated their wages, along with what he would have to pay the government in taxes, based on different number of hours worked, all in his head. He could also calculate the value the person provided the store.

David loved to play all sorts of number games while in the store. He would try to guess how much a person would spend on the items he or she purchased. More times than not, he would be within a few dollars. Of course he knew most of his customers on a first name basis, being a store that catered to the neighborhood.

Two men walked into his store one afternoon. Before anyone could react, one of the men slammed the front door shut and flipped the lock on. David saw the men pull guns from under their shirts. He had installed a silent alarm behind the counter to the police station some months back. Without any sudden movement, he triggered the alarm.

The men told everyone to move away from the counters and stand in the middle of the store. David, his employees and his customers did as they were told. One of the men kept a gun on the small group while the other opened the cash register, emptying the contents.

Suddenly the front glass door shattered. "Police! Everyone freeze!" David dropped to the ground and gunshots scattered all around. A man slumped down next to David. He rolled him on his back and saw blood oozing from his chest. He shielded the man by cuddling his body away from the shots that were still firing. As he held the man, he could feel blood soaking into his shirt. He tried to put pressure on the wound to stem the flow, but it continued filtering at an ever faster rate through his fingers. He felt the life pulse of the warm blood but felt helpless to do anything for the man.

As the gunfire ceased, David could no longer feel breath from the wounded man. His body began to turn cold and lifeless. David continued to hold the man as he watched the robbers carted out of the store by the police.

David heard ambulances pull up. Emergency medical teams entered the store and began working with the remaining victims. One came over to David and pried the man from his arms. They placed him on a stretcher with a blanket over his head and wheeled him out. Another paramedic helped Aaron up and, after checking him over, walked him over to one of the ambulances.

The next thing David knew he was in the hospital. They checked him over again. Physically he was just fine; mentally he was in a daze. He asked about the person who died but no-one would provide information. The police interviewed David while he was still at the hospital. After getting what information they could they told him that someone would place a temporary barricade over the store windows that were broken. A few hours later they let him go.

That evening David could not sleep. The adrenalin that pumped through his body made him pace the floor. His mind would not stop going over the day's events. The actions flashed across his mind, fast and furious. He thought of the values of the groceries, he thought of the value of his employees but every time he thought of the man who died-how could he place a value on life itself? Numbers failed him.

As the next week passed, David began to get the store back into some reasonable order. He felt he needed to do something about the man who died. He went back to the police and asked if they would give him the name and address of the family. They did and he went to see them. The man had a wife and two children. Although in mourning, they let the grocer in. David could not speak, could not find the words he wanted to say, and had trouble even looking at the family. The wife said that they did not hold David in any way responsible for what happened. David left. Tears filled his eyes to the point he could hardly see to walk.

The next day, David decided he still needed to do something. He organized the small merchants in the area to start a fund to financially help the family. Small containers were placed in each store to collect money. On a weekly basis, David collected, counted and placed the contributions in a fund for the family. He would visit the family often, bringing them groceries. Although the family was thankful they said it was not necessary. Over time, David grew to be a part of their family, although he had a family of his own.

David's daily routine helped him return to a normal life, although the thoughts of that dreadful day never departed. He found value in the fund, value in the groceries he delivered to the family, value in helping the children with their homework. David also knew that the value was only real when linked with people. And the value of people cannot be directly measured. Its measurement is determined by a person's place and involvement in their community.

Midrash Bamidbar
In the Wilderness

Micah was the head of a very large firm. His company employed thousands of people and had manufacturing operations throughout the United States. His numerous responsibilities left little time for a wife or family. Micah, although a very successful businessman, and always surrounded by people, felt quite alone in this world.

The daily pressures were starting to bother him. He noticed a brochure that offered a respite from his daily grind. It talked of meditation and finding inner peace on the top of a mountain in the Arizona desert. He decided at the end of the week to take some time off and visit this place.

Micah flew to Phoenix and rented a car to travel to the getaway. It was located in the middle of the wilderness, halfway between Phoenix and Tucson. There were about a dozen people huddled together in a small one-room building. The head of the program was introduced and he explained what would happen over that weekend.

Instructors would teach them the art of meditation. When the students were ready, they would be taken individually to a secluded spot on top of one of the adjacent mountains. They would receive no food or water. The students would fast for forty-eight hours, sit quietly and meditate. The instructors insisted that if they completed the task they would feel refreshed and ready to return to the everyday world, ready to take on any problem.

Micah did not seem thrilled about the program but decided to give it a try, as he needed some way to release his work tensions. With the instructor's guidance, Micah learned to meditate. The next day he was led to a spot on top of one of the neighboring mountains. An instructor sat him on a ledge next to a small opening in the side of the mountain. They called the opening a cave but it was only a small cutout, barely large enough to shield one from the elements. The instructor left and said he would return in two days time.

Micah positioned himself in a lotus position and began to meditate. One hour, then two passed and Micah actually felt pretty good. As the next few hours passed he began to feel hungry. He tried to go into a heavy meditative state but the heat on top of the mountain began to make him sweat and feel uncomfortable. He moved to shield himself inside the cutout of a cave. Although better than the ledge, it was still quite warm.

Try as he might, the meditation did not do the trick. With the onset of night, the heat subsided, but it started to rain. The cave offered little resistance to the downpour. The one saving grace was that he at least could quench his thirst.

With the sunrise, Micah tried again to meditate the day away. Within a few futile hours he decided that this method was just not for him. He stood up and walked down the mountain. As he approached the one room building, the instructors started to scream at him that his time was not up and he would not obtain any benefit from their program trying it for so short a time. Micah ignored them, got into his car and drove away.

As he approached the edge of Phoenix he decided to get off the road and find a place to eat. A few blocks from the freeway exit he noticed a large gathering in front of a building. It was a celebration at a local synagogue. He pulled to the side of the road and got out of his car.

Micah, without knowing why, wanted to get a better look. As he entered the door of the synagogue he noticed the nameplate at the side. It said "Bamidbar Synagogue". Micah thought how appropriate it was for the name of a synagogue at the edge of a wilderness.

It had been a long time since Micah was in a synagogue. He sat at the back. The celebration was a combination Bar Mitzvah and Havdalah ceremony. The sanctuary was packed with people. The service was a mixture of song and chanting. The notes hung in the air and resonated within his body. As the three-fold Havdalah candle was extinguished, ending the formalities, Micah felt a rush of tension leave his body. He seemed refreshed and invigorated.

The father of the Bar Mitzvah boy noticed a stranger in their midst. Micah, not looking so good from his mountain excursion, seemed more like a person in need than a person that held the power of a large corporation. The father invited Micah to stay for the dinner celebration. He said it was the family's tradition to invite a stranger to join their celebration as a mark of hospitality and, if Micah would be so kind to stay, it would be an honor for the family.

Micah stayed. He ate the foods, and even joined the family as they danced and drank the night away. Micah had never felt so good. He did not need to be alone and meditate. He needed to feel as part of a community, part of a family, something apart from his work, and personal. He remembered that although the Jewish people left Egypt for the wilderness, it was not a journey they took alone, but as a family, as a community. That is what was missing from his life. That was the emptiness in him that needed to be filled.

On Micah's return home he sent a thank you note to the family who had been so kind to him at the Bamidbar Synagogue. In the note was a certificate explaining that a large scholarship fund was placed in escrow for the Bar Mitzvah boy to use at the college of his choice, when that time would come. Micah joined a local synagogue. It was not so much the prayers or even the services that Micah enjoyed. It was that he felt a member of the Jewish community. And the loneliness never returned.

Midrash Naso
The Nazir

Joseph was one of those students that just seemed to have everything going his way. He was captain of the football team, always got the best grades and had a number of friends. He was the focus of the whole school and he liked it that way.

People milled around him like he was a movie star. It was Joseph who decided where the next party would be and they would party all night long, with Joseph leading the drinking games, dancing and other nightly activities. Whatever he wanted he simply asked for...and got. It was as if the world orbited around him.

One day in class they talked about the Nazirites. A Nazir was a person who dedicated their life to God in a complete way but only for a short period of time. These people did not cut their hair, drink wine or do things that would make them ritually unclean. The other students made fun of the idea and teased Joseph that he could not possibly be a Nazir, given his lifestyle.

Joseph felt he could do anything. He announced to the class that he would be a Nazir for the next month. He would not drink any alcohol, cut his hair, swear or attend any party. He would not say an unkind word to anyone and to do at least one act a day that would be considered a good deed. The class laughed and took the announcement as a challenge to try to get Joseph to break his vow.

Over the next few days his friends at school began to tease Joseph about his promise. Joseph kept his resolve. He never responded in anger or in any way that would be disrespectful. This only agitated the students even more and within just a few days the whole school began to try to get Joseph to break his vow.

During the next football game, his teammates decided to play a trick on Joseph. He was the running back, and so would often get the ball. As the game was well in hand, his teammates decided to hand the football to Joseph and not block the opposing team. The crunch of Joseph being hit was heard at the top of the bleachers. Joseph simply rose to his feet, brushed himself off and then helped up the opposing players who hit him. Joseph's teammates roared with laughter.

Joseph thought he needed to plan for the good deeds he wanted to do, as he could not be sure that an opportunity would just happen. For the first week he planned the tasks. He helped pick up trash at one of the local parks, donated some time at the animal shelter, and donated clothes he no longer needed to one of the organizations that helped the poor.

During the first part of the month, the students at school made every attempt to upset Joseph. They spray-painted his locker, poked him in the back while going through the halls, and any number of other exploits designed to unnerve him. Joseph was resolved to follow through. He did not fight back, he did not swear, but simply went about his business. He attended no parties and drank no alcohol. As the month went on, the students began to lose interest in Joseph. He was no longer the center of their attention.

As Joseph's hair grew longer, it changed his appearance. The change not only occurred on the outside but the inside as well. Joseph noticed that he could spot when others required help. At school, the girl's swim team needed money to attend a tournament. Joseph went to the neighborhood businesses asking for donations on their behalf and collected enough money to allow them to attend the meet.

176

The local recreation center needed a new coat of paint in the gym. Joseph approached the members of the football team to help out. He was still a leader, but a different sort. His teammates not only painted the gym with Joseph but also donated money for the paint.

When the month ended, Joseph got a haircut. He returned to school but did not return to being the center of attention. Something had changed in him that month. He felt different inside. He was still a leader but in a much different manner. Before it did not matter what the adults felt about him, it was only his friends. His acts were designed to keep him the center of attention, regardless of the results. It was always about him and only him. Now it was different. It was not about him but about them. This made Joseph feel good about himself. It gave him a feeling of being a whole person. This was something he never felt before, and he liked it. He was no longer a Nazir. He was a man.

Midrash Beha'aloscha
How Friends Travel

The ugliness of war can be measured at so many levels. It is not just death that constantly surrounds a person, but the violence, the brutality, the myriad of ways man can demean another man. The battles seemed to never end. Mud caked and exhausted our troop entered the next of the infinite skirmishes.

I rose with my fellow soldiers to move forward as commanded by the troop leader. I heard the zip of a bullet slicing through the air on my left. As in slow motion I saw the bullet rip through the torso of a fellow compatriot. His body folded like an unsupported deck of cards. A second zip caught my ear and again I saw a bullet as it sliced through my left leg, blood and flesh spurting into the air. I collapsed to the ground amidst other fallen soldiers and passed out.

I awoke and found myself lying on a cot underneath a tent like structure. It had a canvas roof but no side walls. My muddy uniform was still draped across my body but the left cloth pant leg had been ripped off and was now replaced with a thick gauze-like wrap. I gazed to the left and then to the right. Wounded soldiers in cots for as far as the eye could see.

Unlike the battle where the noise was constant, loud and deafening, here the silence hung heavy in the air, only to be interrupted by the occasional whimper or moan. At one far end of the tent I could see a set of soldiers stopping by each cot momentarily and then moving on. As they came closer I could tell that they were the enemy, the other side of this war. I was in a prisoner of war camp. The enemy group was composed of a few armed guards, two soldiers passing out food and a doctor who took a quick look at each wounded soldier. When they came to me, the doctor took a look at my leg and said I would be able to work in a few days. Another soldier handed me a few pieces of fruit and a slice of cheese.

The only food that entered my body the past month was field rations- tasteless and bulky but functional enough to provide the dietary needs to keep us going. The taste of fruit sent convulsions across my taste buds. This small supplement would not fulfill dietary needs but it sure did taste good.

After a few days rest a soldier came by, flicked his rifle against my good heel and told me that the doctor approved work detail. I was marched through the ward and into a field of mud.

With other prisoners of war I was required to make bricks by first sifting the mud through a screen to remove rocks and such. I had to then take the sifted mud and mix in straw. Most soldiers used their feet, but my leg was still wrapped in gauze and was stiff and weak. I tried to lift my leg while knee deep in the mud pit but the pain was excruciating. I glanced at an adjacent soldier. He had a gauze wrap as well but his was around his neck. He could not speak. He motioned for me to use my hands instead of my feet. It was messy but I was able to get by.

After mixing the straw with the mud I was to place the material into molds to set. The bricks were removed from the molds and air dried for a few weeks. Other prisoners would take the dried bricks and build structures that would hold supplies, food and other materials the enemy used to conduct the war. Any prisoner not critically ill worked in the mud brick operation.

Time as a prisoner of war meant little. I could not tell if I had been in this form of slavery for four months or four hundred years. Each day was the same. We would rise with the sun, be given a few pieces of fruit, marched to the fields, worked until close to sunset, marched back, given a little more food and flopped in our cots to an exhaustive sleep. Many soldiers succumbed to the monotonous work load, gave up and died.

What allowed me to survive was the friendship developed with the neck injured soldier. We would swap stories daily while in the pits. I would speak mine in as an elaborate fashion as possible and he would use hand gestures to communicate his. It was the highlight of the day and made life bearable. The one quirk was that he would not tell me his name, either through hand motions or by writing it in the mud with a twig. For a few days I would try to guess but he would not reply. So for me friend became his name.

One night it began to rain. Not just the normal shower but the kind that poured down hard. A strong wind slung the rain sideways. As there were no side walls in our tent, the guards were exposed as well. They did not want to remain in the storm so made their way to the inside of one of the mud huts. The moment they disappeared from view my speechless friend rolled over to my cot and motioned me to follow. We slithered through the puddle filled undulating ground until we reached the edge of the adjacent forest. With the cover of the trees we stood and sprinted as fast as his legs and my leg would carry us away from the camp.

Running through a forest in daylight was never an easy proposition. At night it was impossible. Branches lashed at our limbs as we passed. At times those armed creatures landed on my hurt leg. This sent me sprawling and in excruciating pain. My friend picked me up and together we continued to make our way. With sunup we found cover in a small depression in the ground that was covered in thick brush.

Exhausted we spent the better part of the day resting. The time spent as a prisoner created another problem. We were weak from the paucity of food. We would not be able to travel much further without some sustenance. With this understanding, my friend crawled out from the brush, found a long branch stripped of leaves, motioned for me to remain, and with the branch acting as a support staff, walked off into the forest, disappearing in but a few moments.

Too exhausted to move, I laid back and waited. It was not long when my friend reappeared. In one hand he still held the staff, but in the other was some white-grey substance. He crawled back into our hiding place and handed me a piece of what he held. The substance was not quite solid. It was as light as a feather, and jiggled with the slightest movement. White-grey may have been giving this stuff more credit than it deserved. In fact there was no color to it at all. With a hand gesture he motioned for me to take a taste.

I cupped the substance in one hand and moved it slowly toward my mouth. I took a small bite. It had a sweet kind of taste. It took no effort to eat. It dissolved on contact with the inside of your mouth and left a honey like aftertaste. The strangest part was that within a few hours of eating it your energy rose and were ready to travel. Since my friend could not provide a sign for the name of this strange substance I decided to title the stuff myself – Manna!

We spent an extra day hiding in the thick brush, using the time to gain some strength and to see if the guards would come after us. We also needed to pick a direction to travel.

Stories reached the prisoner of war camp of how our allies had captured the tallest mountain in the country and built a large factory on it. The stories claimed that during the day it bellowed out dark smoke and at night fire rose high into the air. The factory could be seen for miles in every direction. That evening my friend climbed a tall tree and behold he could see the fire on the mountain. Even though he could see the mountain and the signs of the factory, it was quite far and in our condition would take many days to travel there, especially through this forest wilderness. The next day we set off for the Promised Land.

Day after day we traveled. On occasion we came across enemy troops. At such times we found a way to conceal ourselves. Sometimes it was thick brush, sometimes in the hollow of a tree, and sometimes by climbing up a tree. These meeting were always nerve wracking as I knew I would not survive a return to a prisoner of war camp.

The most unusual aspect of our journey was that each morning my friend would venture off into the forest and return with Manna to eat. I never saw the stuff as we traveled, nor did I ever get a response as to where he found it. Yet he always did and it always satiated us, refreshed us and gave us energy for travel that day. One time I took a little extra and created a holder for it out of leaves and branches. After traveling a few hours I opened my holder but the Manna was gone. It had disintegrated. I tried to save some a number of times but it would never keep. When my friend brought it back one could consume as much as possible but saving it for a later time was not possible. After many tries I gave up hope to save some of this food for our travel.

Days and then weeks passed. At times the mountain could be seen in the horizon. With all our travel, it did not seem to be getting closer. As for the Manna, the monotony of our diet began to get to me. I saw animals that we might catch for food, but it never happened. I even tried to collect some vegetation to eat. Every time I gathered some of these greens my friend would stop me and indicate that it would be bad in some way for me to consume. At first I listened and then I got mad. "Manna, Manna, Manna – all we eat is Manna! I can't stand it anymore! I think I would rather go back to the prisoner of war camp. At least there we got the occasional piece of fruit!" My friend would listen to my rants, calm me down and we would resume our travel.

My friend had a way to keep count of our travels. He took a piece of flint and sliced a notch in the staff he kept from that first day in the forest, one notch for each day. At night we would stop and rest. At some point during the night my friend would climb a tree and take a bearing to the mountain for our next day's trek.

We had traveled for forty days. On that fortieth day we rounded a bend and came to a river. On the other side but a mile away, the foot of the mountain could be seen and a paved road was visible leading up to the factory.

The river was not deep but the water was swift. To support my bad leg against the current, I placed my arm around the shoulders of my friend and we moved toward the river bank. Upstream an enemy troop came into view and began to move toward us. The forest at this point in the river was sparse and did not allow hiding places. My friend moved me behind the closest tree and gave me his staff. He moved toward the river in sight of the troop and then scampered back into the forest. The troop followed. There was no way to stop him. If I had called out, the troop would have gone after me. As my friend moved into the forest, he turned, smiled and motioned me to cross the river. He would not come with me.

I heard the troop yelling and firing their rifles as they chased my friend. I could not tell if they ever caught him. I forded into the river and used the staff to support me and my wounded leg. I crossed and made it to the road leading to the factory. As I climbed the road, memories flashed across my mind of the mimed stories my friend told me in the mud pits, of the Manna he always came out of the forest with, of the friendship that made life worth living. I never saw my friend again and never did learn his name.

Years have passed. My leg recovered with medical attention. I survived the war, married and had children. I think of my friend often. I tell my children not only the story of our escape to freedom but of the tales we told while in the mud pits. My children had children. They told them these same stories. Memories are not confined to one generation. They remain an indelible part of our future selves, within our children, grandchildren, and generations to come. I am glad that the memory of my friend will live on.

Midrash Shelach
Challah

The very nature of a grandmother makes her special to those lucky enough to have one. The Yiddish term for this relation is Bubbe. The label Bubbe goes beyond the definition of the word. It projects an aura of warmth, love, comfort and a smile that stretches forever.

I have a Bubbe. Her husband died before I was born, so she has lived in our house ever since I could remember. Although I love my mother, there is a different and special tie I have to Bubbe. It transcends anything I could describe and enriches my life in ways difficult to place into words.

It is Bubbe who makes me hot chocolate on an especially cold winter morning. It is Bubbe who plays cards with me when my friends are busy. It is Bubbe who takes me on long walks in the neighborhood or tells me a bed time story. It is Bubbe who simply takes the time to be with me. And it is as important to her as it is to me.

Friday nights are a special time in our family. All our relatives that live in the city descend on our house for a Shabbat meal. Mother is responsible for the main courses. The highlight, however, is always the freshly baked challah. Challah is egg bread, traditional for the Shabbat meal. The smell of baking bread can be detected from the street. The sweet aroma makes your mouth water and the anticipation of taking that first bite is what dreams are made of. It just sort of melts in your mouth and leaves a sweet pleasant taste along with a smile ear to ear.

Bubbe's challah has another unique feature. She always pinches off a little of the dough at the upper side of one end. It produces a little protruding bulb that sticks out at the end of the loaf. When we first sit down to the Shabbat meal, we say a few short prayers. The tradition is for Bubbe to cut the bulb off during the prayer for the bread and give it to someone special.

"Why do you make the little bulb at the end of the loaf, Bubbe?" "In ancient times challah was a portion of the bread set aside for the priests. When the Temple was destroyed, the bread tradition moved into the home as part of the Sabbath meal. The bulb is my way of making the challah into something special. To give the bulb to someone who does a mitzvah is a wonderful way to bring the ancient tradition forward into our own lives. The tradition is changed but is still important."

"Why do you bake so many loaves?" "If you really want to know, meet me after you finish school today." On returning from school we load a number of loaves into the car and begin to drive. Our first stop is the homeless shelter where we drop off a large number of loaves. One of the attendants remarks that she has been doing this for as long as anyone can remember. The bread is so good that the homeless come from all around the city to get a slice or two. We then proceed to the rabbis' house and present him with a loaf. He smiles as she places it in his hands and wishes her and the family a Shabbat Shalom. He whispers, "To me Bubbe's challah is the quintessential start of Shabbat." We make a dozen more stops. The enthusiasm as we exit the car never ceases to amaze me.

This night, as we are about to start the prayer for bread, I motion for everyone to stop. I move over to Bubbe and ask her to give me the knife. Curiously she hands it over. As we start the prayer, I slice the bulb off the end and hand it to her.

Every Friday Bubbe waits for me to come home from school to make her rounds. It is a tradition that I always look forward to. Just before my Bar Mitzvah, Bubbe rouses me from my bed early in the morning and pulls me into the kitchen.

She spends the entire morning teaching me step by step how to make this special bread. At first I try to write the ingredients down but that does not work too well. Her form of measurement is a bissel of this and a bissel of that. Bissel is a Yiddish term for a little. "How can I make this bread if I do not know the exact ingredients?" She says, "It is a labor of love. Love does not have exact ingredients. You must do it by feel!" She grasps my hands into hers and together we roll and knead the dough. "Eggs come big and small, flour changes by batch. But if you know the feel you can always hit the recipe."

My first attempts prove poor. But as the weeks go along, I begin to get what she was talking about. It isn't a sudden thing, like a light that suddenly flashes, but more like an evolution. I knew I finally made it, when on starting to place a particular loaf in the oven, Bubbe saunters over, and with a smile, pinches off the end of the loaf creating her famous bulb.

For many years Bubbe and I would make challah before I went to school and deliver it when I came home. Eventually I grew up, marry and move out of the house. Every week, my wife, children and I go to my father's house, like my other relatives, for the Shabbat meal. However, I no longer bake or deliver the loaves.

Then one night I receive a call from Father. Bubbe passed away. The funeral is a small dignified affair, and very sad. I never noticed before, but the prayer that we say for the dead does not mention death! Our religious tradition tells us that a dead person needs to be placed in the ground as soon as possible. We bury Bubbe one day after she passed away. We sit shiva at my father's house, a seven day period when people come and console the family. There is a steady stream of people from all corners of the city to pay their respects.

I woke very early on Friday morning. The sadness of the week drained me. I miss Bubbe very much, and this Friday would be our first without her. Then it hits me. I jump out of bed and dress as quickly as I can. I kiss my wife and kids and tell them to meet me tonight at father's house for dinner.

I drive over to father's house and begin to bake Bubbe's bread. By midday there are a tremendous number of loaves. I throw them into my car and begin to drive around the city. I stop by every place I could remember Bubbe delivering one of her loaves. I drive to the shelter and drop off loaves. I tell the administrator that the bread would continue to come every Friday afternoon. He thanks me and wishes me a Shabbat Shalom. Stop after stop, the smiles, the warmth, the appreciation, lifts my spirits out of the pale of mourning.

That evening, as we sit for Shabbat dinner, I place a small challah on every plate. Each loaf contains a small protruding bulb sticking out of the end. When we say the prayer, everyone cuts their bulb off and places it on a single plate sitting in the center of the table, a picture of Bubbe at its side.

I am able to take every Friday off by working on Sunday instead. On Friday I rise early, travel to my Father's house and bake challah for our relatives, for our friends and for those in need. When my children are old enough I will teach them how to bake these special challahs with a protruding bulb. They too will join in the delivery around the city. In this way Bubbe will not be just a memory, but someone who lives on in our hearts for generations to come.

Midrash Korach
The Rebellion

John and Barry loved sports. Their favorite to watch and play was baseball. They would sit for hours talking about the major leagues, the pennant races, and statistics, just about anything connected with the sport. In most cases they disagreed and the heated discussions were legendary. Yet on one thing they were in absolute accord: their favorite player was Adam Goldberg, right fielder for the Detroit Tigers.

Adam had all the skills. Swift of foot, he chased down any balls hit in his direction and his fundamentals like hitting the cut-off man was unrivaled. He could also hit. Home runs, singles, and doubles, whatever the need, more times than not he came through. What made him even more special for the boys was that he was Jewish. There were almost no other Jewish major leaguers. John and Barry, being Jewish themselves, looked to Adam as someone who reached the dream they wished for.

It was early fall. School had begun. Fall also meant the beginning of the baseball playoffs, and the Tigers made it to the finals. The winner would go to the World Series. Fans of the Tigers and Adam waited years for them to be this successful and it caused great excitement for those who followed the game.

The series was tied at three games each. The deciding game would be this Saturday afternoon at Tiger Stadium. John and Barry attended all the other home games. Although tickets were expensive, the boys were friendly with one of the ushers, who just happened to be one of their coaches of the school team. Last year, John and Barry led the school to their first state championship, so the coach felt especially fond of the boys. He would look the other way as they scooted over the turnstiles and into the stadium.

There was a problem with the timing of the final game. Although not conflicting with school because it was Saturday, it was going to be Yom Kippur, the Jewish holiday known as the Day of Atonement. The family would be at the synagogue from morning until night. John and Barry did not know what to do. They talked to their parents. They said there was no choice, Yom Kippur took precedence over all other activities.

The boys were crushed. Their whole lives they had
waited for the Tigers to reach this level of success and now they
were going to miss it. The more they talked, the angrier they
got. Didn't their parents realize how important this game was?

John and Barry met after dinner on Friday night. They
tried to think of any way to watch or at least listen to the game.
Perhaps they could pretend to be sick and have to stay home.
They could say they have to go to the bathroom during the
service and sneak back to one of the school rooms that had a
television, or maybe hide a small radio in their suit jacket
pocket and run an earphone into their ear with transparent
tape so their parents couldn't see!

John and Barry talked most of the night. As the hours
passed, the discussion turned to how important the religious
service was for them. John did not have any feeling at all for
Judaism. It was just a label for him. Barry felt a little different.
As he talked about it, he mentioned how he looked forward to
seeing his cousins and other family members. They did not
see each other very often, but always on holidays and he liked
them. He talked about how his mother seemed so happy in
the kitchen preparing for when they broke the fast. The whole
family would be over and the food was always great and
plentiful. Barry pictured his great grandfather, still alive and
kicking, at the synagogue. He had a very peculiar ritual when
he placed a kipa (a skullcap traditionally worn during a prayer
service) on his head and then his tallit (a prayer shawl) around
his shoulders. It reminded him of a slow motion replay of a
great sports play. Barry even thought about the blessings he
says on Yom Kippur and how the family always discussed the
meanings behind the prayers. It was a special day and one he
always looked forward to.

John, even more upset than earlier in the week, vowed to rebel. He would go to the game no matter what. He would sneak out of the house early in the morning and go down to the ballpark. What could his parents do? He would see the game. He would see Adam Goldberg hit one out of the park and win the game for the Tigers. He told Barry he would meet him at six a.m. Barry paused. Baseball was important but the holidays were too, and the choice was difficult. He wanted to see the game but just could not bring himself to sneak out.

At six in the morning Barry slid out of bed and moved over to the window. He could see John exiting his house and began walking past. John motioned one last time for Barry to join him. Barry just shook his head.

Barry and his family left for the synagogue about nine thirty. Although services would not start for another hour the place was packed. People chatted away waiting for the service to start. He picked up different conversations from around the room and many talked about the game. Barry spotted John's parents. They were visibly upset and squirmed a lot in their seats.

Just after services began there was a big stir throughout the congregation. Person after person turned and strained their head to look the back of the room. Barry could not make out what was going on but the Rabbi from the bima (a raised stage like area where the service is led) turned and gave a stern look, quieting the members.

The rabbi approached the microphone and announced that someone very special that year would have the honor of parading the Torah. He called a person's name in Hebrew and someone from the back of the room stood and approached the bima, taking the scroll and turned to begin the march throughout the congregation. Barry had to rub his eyes twice. It was Adam Goldberg.

As Adam passed with the Torah he noticed Barry's kipa with a Tiger's emblem on it. He gave him a friendly wink and moved on. Many congregants mulled around Adam after the first set of services ended. Adam was polite and tried to respond to most everyone. Slowly the synagogue began to empty. Barry and his family were one of the few that spent the full day at the synagogue. He noticed that Adam also remained for some of the smaller afternoon services. As things quieted Adam actually moved over to sit next to Barry and introduced himself. Barry, blushing a dark shade of red, said he knew who he was and mumbled a few more short lines in awe.

As time went on the two began conversing. Barry told him how much he loved to play the game and all about this year's school championship. He told Adam how much he loved the way he played all aspects of the game- not just his hitting but how he was so good at all the fundamentals. Now it was Adam's turn to blush.

Barry asked Adam why he was at the synagogue and not at the game! Adam said how important Judaism was to him. How he made it so much a part of his life. He explained that he always attended Shabbat morning services. When the team went on the road for ballgames he would go to one of the local synagogues. It gave him great pleasure to meet other Jews from around the country and participate in their prayer services. As they were in the morning, the services did not interfere with the afternoon games and the team made sure that travel arrangements were made so he could attend.

Yom Kippur, although not as important as Shabbat, was still something special. Although he wanted to be with his teammates, this was so much a priority for him that he actually wrote into his contract with the baseball team that *he would be allowed to miss a game if a conflict arose.* I know baseball is important, and I know how much the city cares about the team, but we all have to set our priorities and this is one of mine.

Barry and Adam continued to sit, talk and pray together right through closing services. Barry's parents invited him back to the house to break the fast. Adam agreed. After filling up on the variety of delicacies, Adam asked Barry if he had an extra baseball glove, that maybe they could go outside to play a game of catch. By the time Adam had finished the request, Barry appeared with two gloves and a baseball already in hand.

After tossing the ball around for a bit, Adam brought Barry over and showed him how to throw different types of pitches. He taught him the curve, a change-up, and a slider. He then showed him a few batting techniques that might come in handy. Barry absorbed the lessons like a sponge. Barry told Adam how well he teaches the game. Adam asked Barry if he could keep a secret. When his playing days are done he hoped to become a coach.

The night ended and Adam left. Barry and Adam exchanged addresses and Adam promised to stay in touch with his new friend. As for John, his parents were so upset they grounded him for three months. He could not see or talk to friends out of school or participate in any after school activities. It was as if he had been swallowed whole by an earthquake and disappeared.

Through the excitement of the evening Barry forgot to find out what happened in the game. The Tigers lost. It was interesting that the newspaper stories that followed did not blame Adam for not playing. They admired his convictions and knew that without him the Tigers would have never made it as far as they did.

Midrash Chukat
A Big Stick

Daniel graduated college and he did not know what he wanted to do. As a major in English there were not many professions open to him that seemed attractive. A few months passed and he seemed to just be wavering in the wind. He found some information on *Educate America.* It is a group that services areas with poor educational systems, areas enveloped in poverty, by supplying teachers who will commit to working in less than ideal conditions. In return they provide training and an eventual teaching certificate, along with a modest living. Daniel decided to give it a try.

He applied and was accepted. He was placed in a school in the city of Columbus, Ohio. The students in this school came from poor, poverty laden families, who provided little support to their children's education. It was rare for high school students to be working beyond an elementary level.

The training that the *Educate America* group gave him in preparation for this job was good, but he found the techniques quite unusable for his particular set of students. High School was approached as a place to hang-out by the students, a place to pass the time until they could graduate and move on. Anything learned was by accident. Interest in education was some far away concept and they had no idea how it would be of any benefit for their future.

Daniel needed to find some novel approach that would grab the attention of the students. He tried to get input from the administration, but they said to keep things the way there were. At first Daniel went along with the flow.

As Daniel passed down the hall between classes he saw a teacher berating a student. The more the teacher yelled, the more the student cowered on the floor. Daniel approached the conflict. The closer he came, the louder the teacher got. The louder the teacher yelled the angrier Daniel got. By the time he reached the scene, he could not control himself. Daniel picked up the teacher by placing his hands under his armpits and like a barbell lifted him straight off the ground. With great force he thrust the teacher against the lockers ----- crash! The teacher folded up like a loose piece of paper and floated to the floor. The student ran away and Daniel red with rage walked to his next class.

Overnight Daniel mulled over the days' incident and was determined to do something. He did not know if his actions would cause repercussions with the administration. Then it came to him. He knew how to reach the kids.

Normally when Daniel entered his classroom, the students were loud, boisterous and egging each other on. Not today. When Daniel entered, the class came to a deafening silence. They viewed some apparition standing in the doorway. A person dressed in a caftan robe with a long staff, sandals, and hair that stood straight on end.

Daniel slid across the floor to his desk and sprung to the top, allowing him to peer over the class as if standing on a mountain. "Students, today life changes. I bring you a set of rules, a set of behaviors, something called mitzvot. It will be by these rules that you will live. It will be by these mitzvot that you will conduct yourselves. It will be a guide as to how to relate to your family, your friends, and to the rest of the world." Daniel unfurled a scroll looking object with some 613 rules and regulations. He spoke them one at a time and asked the students to respond if they understood. The punishment for not following these mitzvot would be decided by the class and carried out by the class. By the end of session they had gone over them all and the students agreed to abide by them.

The exertion overcame Daniel. He called in sick the following day. At the end of the school day the principal called Daniel. His class had taken the substitute teacher and chased her out of the room. They had turned the class upside down claiming it was their right under the rules Daniel had set, something called mitzvot. The principal told Daniel, regardless of his condition, that the following day he had to come to school, talk with these students and return them to some semblance of normalcy.

The next day Daniel entered the room first thing in the morning, dressed in the same caftan. This time the class was not silent. They were the typical loud, boisterous group they were in the past, and did not even give him the slightest notice. Daniel moved to a position on top of the desk. The students still did not calm down. Once again his anger rose. Daniel took his staff and smashed it against the top of the desk. Splinters from the staff and desk flew into the air. The staff was now half its original size and ended with a sharp point. Daniel's rage caught the class off guard. Most fell into their chairs. All were now quiet. Daniel came off the desktop, grabbed the mitzvah scroll and lit it on fire in the middle of the room. He said that if the students wished to die in the squalor of their current condition he would no longer stop them. They did not deserve these rules. They were only for people that cared, people that wished to make something of themselves and their community. This group did not deserve such a way of life.

The students watched silently as the scroll now on fire turned to ash and ended in a pile in the middle of the floor. Daniel took what was left of his staff and smashed the middle of the ashen pile sending flakes careening through the room.

The students, dumbfounded and scared, asked Daniel for forgiveness. They would learn to control themselves. They asked him to please give them back the scroll and the mitzvot. He said he would think about it and left for the balance of the day. He did not know if he could return or extend the energy needed for these students. Yet the next day he did go back to school.

He and the students rewrote the scroll with the 613 mitzvot and all promised to keep them this time around. The rest of the year went well. This class learned more than any previous set of students and went on to be the most successful class in the High School. The idea of the scroll and the mitzvot were passed on to future classes. They too accepted them and the school became a model for other systems in similar dire straits.

After a few successful years Daniel was brought to a meeting of the school board. A position had opened up as principal in one of the neighboring schools. He would not be considered for the position as they could not be sure of he could control his anger based on the smashing of his desk and the incident with the other teacher and the lockers that first year. He was a great teacher but would not be allowed to lead the school as a principal.

Daniel had many more years of teaching success. His methods were studied, written about and copied in many other schools. After many years, he felt tired and ready to retire. He did not have another year of teaching in him. His replacement would be with him as an understudy for the last half of the year. On the last day of school, Daniel took his caftan off and handed it and the staff to the next teacher. Daniel walked out of the school never to be heard of again.

Midrash Balak
The Blind Leading the Blind

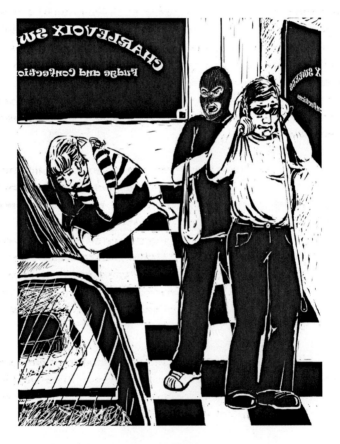

Summer in Charlevoix, Michigan is a quiet pleasant affair, located at the top of Lower Michigan. A small vacation city nestled between Lake Michigan and a smaller inlet lake, it offers cool breezes against a warm summer sun, the sound of small waves lapping at the shore and people enjoying a time away from the grind of work.

The city itself is only five to six blocks long, a few blocks wide, and lined with shops and stores serving visitors that comes up for the summer. Chamor, one of those visitors, sauntered down these streets, doing a bit of shopping. His way of looking at products was different because Chamor was blind. He used touch and sound to examine a store's contents. The products sold by this particular establishment he could tell from the street outside. It made fudge, a staple of the city. The sweet pungent smell could be detected from up to a block away, if the wind was travelling in the right direction. Chamor entered the store.

A second person followed him in. He could tell this not only from the steps of that individual but the clanging of the bells as the entrance door opened. There was something not quite right. Nervousness pervaded the room. "This is a robbery, no-one move". The robber directed the teller to open the cash register and give him all the contents within. The teller obliged. The store owner said, "Even though you are masked, the police will find you and you will go to jail." The robber chuckled and said, "That may be the best thing that could happen to me."

The robber noticed the blind man and took him as a hostage. "If anyone in the store calls the police in the next four hours, the blind man will be killed." He grabbed the back of Chamor's shirt and led him out of the store.

The two proceeded down the street. The robber had one hand on his gun and the other grasping the shirt, directing Chamor down the road as if he were riding a donkey. Chamor suddenly stopped. "Get going, blind man", said the robber. "I wouldn't suggest that", said Chamor. "Why not", asked the robber. "There is freshly poured cement directly in front of us.

If we proceed we will both be covered in the loose cement",
said Chamor. The robber took a look at the path in front and
saw the loose cement and a plastic cover on the walkway.
"How could you possible see this, you're blind!" asked the
robber. I heard the flapping plastic on the walkway against the
gurgle of setting cement", said Chamor. The robber led
Chamor to the right, around the wet cement and then back
onto the walkway.

One-half block later again Chamor stopped. The
robber said, "What is the problem now, blind man?" "I do not
wish to fall down into the hole in front of us." "I see no hole,"
said the robber. "I hear straw moving against the wind and it is
a hollow sound. I also smell loose dirt. This means there is
some sort of construction where a hole was dug in the
sidewalk." The robber took his foot and moved aside some of
the straw revealing a hole beneath, six foot deep. The robber
led Chamor around to the left of the hole and then back onto
the sidewalk.

As the two moved outside the city, once again Chamor
stopped. This angered the robber, who took his gun and hit
Chamor on his back multiple times. Chamor crashed to the
ground, folding up in a ball, wailing against the whipping.
"Why do you hurt me when I have only helped you?" "You
try my patience", said the robber. "Just look at what is in front
of you", said Chamor. The robber peered over the
outstretched body. He saw that the drawbridge had risen to the
point that they could not pass over. If they had continued but a
few more steps they would have fallen into the lake. In the
robber's continued vigilance in looking back over his shoulder
for anyone that might be following, he had not noticed what
was just in front of him. "How did you know the bridge was
up", asked the robber. "My walking stick felt no metal of the
bridge, only the concrete foundation", said Chamor.

The robber sat on the ground next to Chamor, listless, despondent, and silent. "If you do not mind a question, why does a person rob a fudge store? They could not have much money, given their type of business," asked Chamor. "I needed some money, any kind of money. I have not eaten in a few days. I have lost my job, lost my family, and lost all my money. I am hungry and I am desperate. It seemed like an easy place to get enough for a meal", said the robber.

"I am curious about something. With everything that has gone wrong in your life, have you ever turned to God, to your religion", asked Chamor. "Why should I seek out God? I have been a good person, a good husband, a good worker, but I am still have such troubles... I believe in no religion, I can see no God," said the robber.

"I will make you a deal. Give me what you took from the store and I will return it. From my money I will give you enough for a meal tonight. Meet me on the bluff over the city tomorrow at noon", said Chamor. "Why don't I simply take your money as well", said the robber. "You certainly have the ability. Yet perhaps you will trust me just enough to give it a try", said Chamor. The robber thought a few minutes, reached into his pocket and gave Chamor the stolen money. Chamor in turn reached into his pocket and gave the robber money for a meal. The robber turned and left.

At noon the next day the robber met with Chamor on the bluff. Chamor, even though he was blind, could see what the robber needed. Chamor said that he could return the robber's faith in God. From this high place the robber looked around. He turned to see the forest and smelled the pine forests that spread off this high spot. He looked up to the sky and saw majestic clouds, a bright sun and a cooling breeze.

The vistas surrounding this scene included Lake Michigan encompassing the view right to the horizon. It was all very majestic, very spiritual. "Nature is amazing. But it does not feed the belly or provide a roof over one's head", said the robber.

"The majesty of our world in many cases seems like it is God given. But I am blind. I do not see such things. More often than not people look in the wrong places. Instead of looking up or to the horizon, why not look down", said Chamor. At the base of the bluff was a synagogue. On the window of the entrance a sign could seen. It said 'Help Wanted'. "I was talking the other day with a congregant from that synagogue. They mentioned that a janitor position was available", said Chamor. "That is not much of a job", said the robber. "You are right, but it is a start. It will be enough to pay some bills, put a roof over your head and help you to eat. While you are working there you can search for something you prefer as a profession", said Chamor. "It is a new beginning not a dead end."

Chamor said, "Judaism is about community, it is about people living together. It is about people helping each other. I am sorry you have had a rough time. But together we can start to build. That is far more majestic and beautiful than these lakes, the clouds and the trees. You have a chance to begin a new life."

Midrash Pinchas
The Inheritance

Barry and Becky were thrilled when their first baby was about to be born. Family was everything to them. Something went wrong during the delivery and although baby and mother survived, Becky would never be able to get pregnant again. Their child was a healthy, beautiful baby girl, and they named her Rachel.

Their prized possession was a large Tanach, a Hebrew Bible that was as an heirloom passed down from generation to generation for as long as anyone could remember. The heavy book had a dark blue cover trimmed in gold. The pages were thick and yellowed with age. The letters within were large and ornate.

There were two traditions that went with this book. Anyone in the extended family that had a Bar Mitzvah would read one line out of this book on the bimah when reciting their Torah portion, with the remainder, of course, to be read from a Torah scroll. Second, the book was inherited through the eldest male child. That is how it came to be in Barry's possession. In his house there was a crystal glass cabinet that held the book on a stand. It remained in this sealed container with the exception of the times when it was used by any male family member at the synagogue for a Bar Mitzvah.

Barry had one brother, named Sam. He was married and had three children, the oldest a boy named Absalom, who happened to be born the same year as Rachel. The families would gather for holidays and an occasional weekend. Although no one spoke of it, some friction developed between Barry and Sam, because Sam assumed it would be his son who would eventually inherit the family Tanach.

Rachel had a very close relationship with her father. They spent hours together doing all manner of things. They liked to play a trivia game whose topics always came from the Tanach. Rachel had a real affinity for Hebrew and enjoyed studying Judaism. When she was young, the trivia was simple and straightforward. But as she grew, the topics became harder so that even Barry had to spend time pouring through the text looking for questions to ask and trying to find answers to questions posed by his daughter.

Absalom was about to turn thirteen. In the last family get-together Sam surprised the family by announcing that Absalom's Bar Mitzvah would not be held at the synagogue but at the Western Wall in Israel. As a present to the family, Sam would buy all the airplane tickets for the whole family to go over. He asked that Barry bring the family Tanach on the trip so his son could read his first line from it, as generations before had done.

Barry's excitement for the trip to Israel was soon replaced by remorse and regret. The cherished heirloom would soon be gone. To make matters worse, Absalom did not take the Bar Mitzvah, or for that matter Judaism itself, seriously. It was a game to be played, going through the motions to obtain rewards. Religion did not have a place in his life.

Rachel felt much the same way as her father but for a different reason. Girls in the family never had a Bat Mitzvah. It just was not done. Her love for Judaism made her wish she would be allowed to read from the Torah at the synagogue. Her happiness to go to Israel, like her father, was replaced by a deep sadness.

The trip overseas was uneventful. The family spent the first few days sight-seeing in Jerusalem. Everyone was having a festive time, but as the Bar Mitzvah day approached, the sadder Barry and Rachel became. The day arrived and the family walked through one of the large gates leading into the Old City. Barry had the family Tanach in hand.

As they approached the Western Wall the girls split off from the men. A cloth barrier was erected to separate the sexes who would pray at the Wall. The family met at a place near the Western Wall close to the barrier so that the women would be able to hear Absalom recite the Torah portion.

As the men huddled and Absalom began to recite the prayer before reading from the Torah, Barry noticed how nervous he looked. Sweat poured from his forehead, a sour, frightened look plastered across his face. The book from which he read the opening prayer shook in his hands.

Barry opened the large family Tanach to the page of Absalom's reading. He had other family members help hold the book steady because of its size. Absalom approached the Book and located the line. He opened his mouth but no words came out. He tried to compose himself and restart. Again no words came forth. A third attempt, and a third failure. Absalom crumbled to the ground, his body slumped in utter exhaustion.

The women, being able to hear but not see, seemed confused by what was happening. Barry whispered to his wife through the cloth barrier what had happened. Suddenly a female voice, loud, clear and steady began to recite the passages from the Torah. Barry looked at Sam. Both knew who sung the lines. Rachel, eyes closed, recited not only the opening and closing prayers but the entire Parasha by heart.

Sam moved over to Barry and took the Tanach. As the family left the Western Wall, Sam took Rachel's hand and together they moved to an area adjacent to the Wall. Large Jerusalem stones were scattered on the ground. Sam spread the Tanach on top of one of the stones, opened it to the correct page and motioned for Rachel to come forward.

The family congregated around the stone. Sam placed a head covering on Rachel and motioned for Barry to place a prayer shawl over her shoulders. He asked her to recite. Rachel sang the opening prayers and then, eyes focused on the Tanach, chanted the line from the large, blue book. Sam then closed the Tanach and opened a Torah scroll. Rachel continued to read from the scroll, a yad (a pointer used so as not to touch the parchment with your hands) held firmly in her hand. The sounds were loud, clear and beautiful.

Sam closed the Torah scroll and handed it to another family member. He then raised the heirloom above his head displaying it to the rest of the family and handed it to Rachel. He smiled at Barry, shook his hand and went back to the hotel.

Barry was shocked and stunned. The significance of the day did not quite hit him until later. The tradition had changed. His daughter would inherit the heirloom. Rachel had kept the book clutched in her arms as if it were a precious baby, while the whole family traveled back to the hotel.

Barry and Rachel sat together in the hotel room, quiet and subdued, the Tanach placed on a table. Rachel exclaimed how beautiful the cover was and began to run her hands over the bindings. In the lower cover of the back inside binding she felt a bulge. This was unusual as the book was of such high quality that an imperfection would not have been expected. She examined this bulge a little closer and it turned out to be a small latch. She motioned for her father to see and with his consent she turned the latch. The inside cover was actually a small door that opened to a compartment.

Within the compartment was a piece of parchment. Rachel carefully removed the parchment and opened it up. It contained the names of her descendants that went back to the early Middle Ages. Written there were the names of all members of the family that had possessed the book. Strangely, it stopped about three generations back.

The next day, Rachel and her father went to the Old City and found a Torah scribe. They had a new piece of parchment made with the names of the family members who had the book from three generations back to the present. The following day they brought the entire family together and showed them the secret compartment and what was contained within.

Barry took the original parchment and spoke out loud the names of the family members that had possessed the book. He then called his brother up and handed him the new parchment, asking him to recite the names. He began with the missing generations. He then spoke his brother's name, Barry, then Rachel, and then paused. Tears began to stream down his cheeks and in a voice cracking with emotion spoke his own name and that of his son Absalom. Barry took both the aged and new piece of parchment and placed them back into the book's compartment, relatching the cover. A few days later, Rachel took Absalom's hand and led him back to the Old City. There as the whole family gathered, Absalom read confidently and clearly from the Torah.

Midrash Mattot
The Oath

Elijah was an excellent student. He loved to learn but most of all he loved to apply what he learned. He was quite young when he made the decision to become a doctor. It was the perfect profession for the kind of person he was.

Elijah made it through medical school with no problem. He was near the top of his class. The day came to graduate. At the end of the ceremony, the Dean motioned the class to rise and repeat the Hippocratic Oath. Most of the day was a blur but Elijah remembered two things about that oath. The first was that the Dean called it a type of covenant. Elijah remembered from his Jewish education that a covenant was a deal, a contract. In contracts there are at least two parties and each are required to do something on behalf of the deal. Elijah reached back to his educational roots and remembered that an oath was a sworn affirmation to be true and faithful to one's promises. He remembered that a covenant was a solemn promise between two parties. Who were the two or more parties in the Hippocratic Oath? The doctor was certainly one, but who was the other? The other phrase that seemed to resonate deep within Elijah was "to do no harm". This was plain, simple and straight forward. It was a guiding principle and one he certainly believed in.

Elijah decided he would become a diagnostician at a hospital. What better profession than to apply everything he had learned. Elijah was a good doctor and worked at his profession for a number of years. The oath he took on graduation day remained at the forefront of his thoughts and he helped save many lives.

Elijah received a call from the emergency room. They asked him to come in and look at a peculiar case. A pregnant woman had been rushed to the hospital with severe back pain. She had a little bleeding and the baby was not moving at all.

Elijah did an initial exam and then ordered a number of other tests, making sure those tests would not impact the unborn child. He found that the mother had a case of placental abruption, a condition in which the placenta separates from the uterus before the baby is born. This is serious in that the baby may not receive enough oxygen or nutrients. It can also cause severe bleeding which is a risk to both baby and mother. Back pain is a symptom of the condition but the way the pain manifested itself gave Elijah cause to check further. Additional investigations found a mass pressing against the spine of the mother. The baby was right at term, the pregnancy lasted just about nine months. Tests indicated that at least at this point the baby was fine.

This caused a major quandary. They needed to operate on the mother immediately to remove the mass or it would certainly kill her. However if they operated to remove the mass it might kill the baby. If they tried to take the baby by c-section prior to the operation it might kill the mother.

The only thing that kept creeping into Elijah's thoughts was that medical oath he had taken so long ago- do no harm... Elijah tried to use every bit of his prior training to resolve this tricky matter. He turned to his Jewish roots. The Talmud said that an unborn child has the status of "potential human life" until the majority of the body has emerged from the mother. Potential human life is valuable, but it does not have as much value as a life in existence. The Talmud was quite blunt. If a fetus threatens the life of the mother, the mother is saved. But once the greater part of the body has emerged, its life cannot be taken to save the mother's, because a person cannot choose between one human life and another.

In this case it was not the baby that threatened the mother but an issue with the mother itself. And although the baby was not yet born, it could be at this point in time. An ultrasound showed a fully developed baby. Monitors of the baby's heart blood pressure and remainder of the vital signs indicated a fully healthy individual. Jewish law says that the mother may take precedence, yet Elijah knew there was a healthy human in that womb waiting for a chance at life. This was a case when someone would have to be harmed to save the other and it conflicted and confused Elijah. He did not know the right choice to be made.

The hospital tried to reach the husband or another relative. It was Elijah's hope that he or they might shed some additional light on the situation providing some direction for a decision. No relation could be found. Then the mother began to bleed more profusely. They needed to act. Elijah remembered a story he read about a Jewish family in World War II. The family had been captured by the Nazis. They brought the two parents and a thirteen year old child into a room. They turned to the child and said that one parent would be shot and the other would live. The child would have to choose which parent would die. The agony was so terrible that the child rushed to attack the Nazi guard nearby and was shot dead. In this way the child avoided having to make such a terrible choice. There would be no such out in this case. Even if Elijah could choose himself to die, it would not change the medical situation.

Most people think that being a doctor means always to make such decisions. This is far from reality. In most cases doctors act as human mechanics. They analyze the broken part and either patch or replace the part. The vast majority of cases are mundane, routine and a function of guessing which test to run in order to get the right information. In some cases even when the information indicates that there is nothing to be done for the patient and the patient may soon die, there is little the doctor has to decide on. Certainly how to tell the patient comes into play but in most cases even this becomes straight forward and repetitious.

It was then that Elijah remembered the introduction of the oath he took, the part about the covenant. Perhaps the other parties to the oath could weigh in on this matter. But who were the other parties? He decided to approach the pregnant woman. Perhaps in this case she should have a say in such an ominous choice. The mother was delirious and the few drugs they could use because of her pregnant condition made her unable to provide any coherent response.

Elijah journeyed to the chapel. Perhaps God would be a partner in this decision? Religiously the covenant was in fact a partnership between us as a person, and as a people, and God. Elijah prayed. Elijah prayed. Elijah prayed. No answer came to him. No voice was heard. Elijah clenched his fist harder and harder, hoping for some help, hoping for a direction. He could feel the sweat streaming down his forehead.

"Elijah, Elijah, wake up!" Elijah stirred and opened his eyes. Over his prone body he saw his wife standing over him, a concerned expression over her face. "Elijah I have been trying to wake you. It is time!" Elijah responded- "Time for what?" "The baby silly. I am in labor. We need to go to the hospital. It is time for this baby to be born!" Through his recovering stupor, Elijah began to remember. He looked around and found he was in his bed. His wife asked him why he was sweating so and why his fists were clenched so hard while he was sleeping. Elijah simply responded that he was asking God to answer a question. She asked if God did. Elijah simply smiled, exhaled a relieved sigh and responded with a nod of approval.

Midrash Masei
The Journey

Al's life may be described as one surrounded by turmoil. It was not Al himself but those around him that were embroiled in issues. The turbulent vortex of those individuals somehow spun Al into the middle of these problems. It was Al's way to provide calm, direct solutions.

Al was a child of The Depression. His father found work when he could and food was often scarce in his large family of brothers and sisters. His father had a soft heart and would often take in children from broken families and provided what food and shelter he could. This meant even less for Al, already receiving a meager amount for a growing boy. Yet it provided a base of understanding that informed his life as an adult. And the journey continued.

Al went to school as a youngster but it meant little. It was after school that most interested him. It was in this time frame that he would search for any odd jobs to make a little extra money. The money he made never went into his own pockets but to help his family. He liked to work and he could work long hours without tiring.

One time Al and his brother walked into a shop on the remote outskirts of town and asked the owner if he needed any help. The owner asked the boys he either knew how to drive a car as he needed someone to move some supplies from his farmhouse to the shop. If one of the boys could drive, he would pay them to transport the material and lend him his car to do so. Simultaneously both answered they could drive and would be happy to lend a hand. Of course neither had been behind the wheel before. They often watched their own father do it and felt they could muddle through. Besides it would be fun. Al got behind the wheel and although the car jerked along, they were able to do the job. And the journey continued.

Growing up Al tried many lines of work. He was very observant and learned from others while doing these odd jobs. He was often able to pick up work at construction sites. They always needed cheap labor to help pick up and move materials. Al spent as much time as he could with different workers at the sites. Painters, electricians, carpenters, people who poured the cement foundations – all knew Al was a good worker, was affable and they liked how hard he tried. Because the workers liked Al they indulged his constant questioning about how they did their trades. As he grew, he learned and became very good at most any job. And the journey continued.

Soon The Depression ended but World War replaced the former turmoil with just another dangerous vortex. As Al was a young man, he was drafted into the army. He learned to be a soldier in the same easy way he learned other trades. His makeup and education would not move him into the ranks of leadership. He was one of many soldiers who faced the front lines of battle as a private. The war swirled and Al saw soldier after soldier die around him. He too would not be lucky enough to avoid the flying metal that seemed ever present. He was crossing a bridge when a bullet hit his leg right at the knee. He fell to the side, off the bridge and toward the river below. In those few split seconds he remembered that for all he had learned growing up, swimming was not one of those skills. He hit the water and began to sink. He felt a tug at his clothes and his body rose out of the water. Another soldier had grabbed him and dragged him to shore. He was brought to a field hospital where doctors removed the bullet and patched him up. Al somehow survived the remainder of the war and finally went home. And the journey continued.

Al returned to doing odd jobs. He met a girl and fell in love. The first few years were wonderful but fate began to swirl again. His wife became pregnant but during the delivery there were complications and the child died. Of the multitude of problems Al faced up to this point in his life, this one took the wind out of his sails. Yet he persevered, he survived, and the journey continued.

The vortex returned, and his wife contracted Hodgkin's disease. Al and his wife lived in the north and the winter cold exacerbated his wife's condition. They decided to winter in Florida. They found a small inexpensive place right on the ocean. Al was able to support them through doing odd jobs for the multitude of apartment buildings that dotted the area. In winter these places were packed with snowbirds, winter residents that spent the colder months in these sunny climes. There was never a shortage of jobs.

It was dusk that Al liked best. He and his wife would unwind from the hectic day by sitting on the beach and watching the sunset. The crash of the waves on the shore washed away every bit of anxiety, every bit of turmoil the day created. Life being what it was for Al, the vortex returned, and his wife succumbed to the disease. There would be no more winters in Florida. The thought would be too painful. And the journey continued.

Al returned to the north. Work soothed his psyche. He took a job as a factory troubleshooter at an automotive firm. On the side he built houses. Work would last sixteen hours a day. He would go home and fall asleep while eating a little something. Somehow within this hectic schedule he found another wife, one that had a little girl from a previous marriage where the husband also died of a medical condition. Al now had a family. He continued to work long hours but that was just his way. And the journey continued.

The concept of family was different in Al's world. One of his work associates at the automotive plant died in a freak accident. His friend had one child, a thirteen year old boy. The mother had passed away years earlier from Hodgkin's disease, which was the common link that brought these two together in the first place. No relative stepped forward to take the child in. Al opened up his house, and gave this child a place to live and grow up. He did not formally adopt this child but opened up his home and treated him no differently than he did his own child. Al was always distant in his relationships with people, yet for children he felt a special draw. He saw the turmoil in their lives and sought to provide a worthy ship to traverse the issues in life. He always lent a helping hand, often anonymous, some gesture that lifted child after child from their own vortexes. And the journey continued.

Al's little girl from the second marriage was treated as if she were his own. This little girl grew up and married. Grandchildren soon came on the scene. In most cases the vortexes in Al's life were dangerous and sad. The swirl caused by grandchildren was just as dizzying but could only bring a smile onto Al's face and warmness throughout his body. One day a grandchild opened a kitchen pantry, took out a bottle of cooking oil and spilled the contents all over the kitchen floor. Grandmother and grandchild slid and slipped about the kitchen unable to get out. Al, seeing the precarious situation, grabbed a broom handle and held it out into the kitchen. Grandmother and grandchild grabbed hold of the stick and Al swung them around like an amusement park ride. And the journey continued.

The extended family often traveled together. They took little car trips to places they had never been. Al, silent most of the time, absorbed the action as the grandchildren ran and scurried and bounced through whatever locale they were at. It was strange that the chaos of life seemed always present but shifted in how it was perceived. And the journey continued.

Life moved steadily onward. Al and his wife grew old, and like an old automobile, their parts started to give out. There would be no more running, walking was hard enough. There would be no more trips. The body could not take it and the mind could not comprehend. Al's wife slipped one day and broke her hip. A few months later she passed away. Al, though still able to muddle around, slowly lost his ability to remember. At first it was short term stuff, but slowly, ploddingly, even long term memory faded. It is strange that the short term memory goes before the long, but in the end Al could not even recognize his grandchildren. Then one long winter evening, Al passed away. The vortex of life stopped. The journey ended.

Children, grandchildren, friends, and associates, gathered to remember Al. What would be his inheritance? What would he pass to those who surrounded his life? He saved only a few dollars from all his hard work across the years. Most of what he earned went to doctors, the support of his family and charity to others. Usually at this time a person has his estate documented, enunciated and distributed. Houses, cars, money and other property are listed like an auctioneer's voice, a final word defining a person's life. A will is a document built on material possessions, a tower reaching to the sky, like Babel.

But for Al there would be no such oration. At his memorial service the multitude of people he had helped over the years came and in silent honorarium, much like the person they were there to pay homage to, stood as his final will and testament. If the expression is true that to save one person is to save the world, then Al had saved many worlds. It was his inheritance that they lived and not only withstood the dangerous vortexes of life but excelled and led others down similar paths. Al's journey had ended but his inheritance lived for generations to come.

Midrash Devarim
The Legacy

David Moreh was fresh out of college and wanted to start his own business. His specialty was teaching reading and writing skills to mentally disabled children. He developed a whole variety of techniques from computer programs to physical exercise games that taught these children enough for them to be able to read a book or magazine and understand what was on the page.

David settled in a small suburb outside of Detroit. He was hired at a small school that paid him a salary barely enough to live on. Yet David was happy. Throughout the week he worked with twelve children. His teaching techniques proved very successful.

David was contacted by a school in a neighboring suburb that also catered to these types of children. They asked if he would be interested in a similar position with their organization. David talked with the first school and was able to work out a schedule without having to cut back on hours, and therefore salary. The ability to service two schools increased his pay to where he was making a decent living. David was now teaching up to twenty-five kids per week.

A year went by. David's teaching techniques had proved so successful that his reputation grew. With the start of a new school year, many parents tried to enroll their disabled children in David's classes. His students doubled. At first he tried to divide his time in order to reach them all. He worked nights and weekends to keep up with the load, but within weeks it started to wear on him. Although each of the students received what they needed, David was exhausted and clearly in need of some rest. To rest would mean cutting back and not teaching students who needed his help.

Things went from bad to worse. His reputation continued to spread and other schools wanted to employ his techniques. Parents, desperate for any help, tried to get David's current schools to enroll their child. Many were turned away because there was no more room. They were upset and disconcerted.

David needed help and needed it fast. He could not take on more students and could not keep up his current pace. He came up with a plan. He picked twelve colleagues that believed in his program. He took the next month teaching them his techniques and then spread them out throughout the school system.

For the most part the solution worked. The school system was able to handle students in the city that had these special needs. A few years had gone by and David was able to settle into an acceptable routine. So much so, he was able to actually plan a vacation. He wanted to go somewhere quiet, somewhere remote, somewhere far away from the hustle and bustle of this city. He chose a small town about fifty miles outside of Cheyenne, Wyoming. There was no hotel but they did have a small Bed and Breakfast. He would take a week and soak up the sun, take long walks and just clear his mind.

The week finally arrived. He boarded a plan, flew to Cheyenne, rented a car and drove to his remote Shangri-La. Every day after breakfast he sauntered outside and took a long walk, picking a new direction without rhyme or reason.

It was on the third day of this bliss that he passed a small school building. He stopped and watched the kids in the playground running and jumping and playing. A man standing in the playground saw David and came over to see this person who was just standing and watching. They did not get strangers around this village and such an oddity raised questions. "Is there something I can help you with?" asked the man. Startled David responded, "Excuse me?" "I am the Principal of this school and we don't see strangers around here too often. I was wondering about your business here?" asked the man. "I am here on vacation and was just taking a walk when I passed your school. My job back home is connected with schools and I just stopped to watch. I meant no harm." responded David. "And what is your name sir?" asked the Principal. "My name is David Moreh. I am from a suburb outside of Detroit." "Not THE David Moreh – the one who developed the system for helping disabled children?" "Yes, I am. How did you know my name?" The Principal grabbed David's arm and led him inside the school. Through the window of a classroom David saw his techniques applied to the students. The Principal had read in a number of Journals about David's techniques and contacted some of the other teachers back east who were applying them. From them they learned how to use David's approach. These teachers in turn have taught a number of other teachers around the State on how to use David's techniques. If he did not know it, his method was now used in most school systems around the country.

David was recognized as the leader in his field but did not realize the extent his work had travelled. The government recognized this achievement and was to present David a major national award. The award came with money and facilities to extend his teaching techniques worldwide. The night before the award ceremony, David passed away in his sleep.

Friends, colleagues, teachers and people in his field gathered for the ceremony. A presenter spoke to the crowd and told them of David's untimely death. Many speeches were given honoring David for his work. The original twelve teachers banded together to form an association. The money from the award was used to train more teachers and continue to expand the use of David's techniques. From such a small start David had touched many lives. His techniques, his legacy, would extend far into the future.

Midrash Vaeschanan
The Mezuzah

It was moving day. Dan and his father left their house for the last time. As they passed through the front door, Dan's father stopped, took a small knife from his pocket and carefully pried a mezuzah from the doorframe. Dan had never really noticed the mezuzah before and twisted his head in curiosity. Dan's father saw the quixotic look, kissed the mezuzah and handed it to Dan. He asked him to hold it safely until they reached the new house.

Dan asked his father why they placed a mezuzah on the door. He smiled and responded in as kind a voice as Dan could ever remember. He said there were two meanings. The first was to remind us to always think of the mitzvot, good deeds, that the Torah says we should do for all. The second was as a visible sign to the world that we are Jewish, and proud of our heritage. Dan's father took out and unfolded the parchment that was found within the mezuzah and explained what it contained.

Dan's father asked him how he felt being Jewish. Dan said he had not really thought about it. It was just something he accepted, not unlike knowing that he was a boy. Yet Dan had a certain amount of pride and being Jewish was part of who he was. When they arrived at the new house, Dan and his father placed the mezuzah on the doorframe. His father said a prayer and together they entered their new house.

The incident had left an indelible impression on Dan. As he traveled around the city for one reason or another, he found himself glancing at the doorframes as they passed by. On occasion he would spot a mezuzah. When they went to the synagogue he noticed their mezuzah. Mezuzahs come in all sizes and shapes. Each time he saw one it was as if there was a connection, something familiar and welcoming.

Walking with some friends in a shopping area, Dan noticed a mezuzah on the doorframe of a small clothing shop. He went in and introduced himself to an older couple, the owners of the establishment. He wanted to tell them that he thought their mezuzah was very nice. The man thanked him and proceeded to have a conversation with Dan that lasted for over an hour. At its end the gentleman and his wife invited Dan over Friday to have a Shabbat meal with them. Dan thanked them and did so.

The experience was so nice that Dan started getting into the habit of unannounced visits when he saw a mezuzah on a house or business. There were times that the people within did not take kindly towards the surprise intrusion on their lives. But for the most part Dan was welcomed and made new friends and acquaintances easily. It opened up whole new worlds and the Judaic connection always seemed to bridge the unfamiliarity and awkwardness that usually accompanied introductions to new people.

Dan's father was to travel to Europe on business and decided to take his family with him as a vacation. After his father's business was concluded the family rented a car and traveled through northern France, not too far from the German border. It was Friday and they decided to stop in one of the small towns.

On entering the city they noticed a small synagogue. The family wanted to attend services and thought it would be fun to go into a place they did not know. The synagogue was small, holding not more than a few hundred people. It was warm and quaint. The service was done mostly in song and the tunes were familiar to Dan and his family. Without knowing a word of the local dialect, they managed to feel at home in this part of the globe, so far from their home. After the service, the congregants welcomed the family and found ways to communicate even though they did not know each other's language. It was a very pleasant Shabbat.

Sometime in the middle of the night Dan and his family was roused from their sleep by the clanging of fire trucks rumbling through the streets. They could see a large blaze, a holocaust, towering high into the sky.

The next morning, the family walked to where the fire had been. It was the synagogue. The building was nothing but a pile of cinder. A few beams remained of the outer framing but even they were charred beyond repair.

On the grass front of the burned out building was a sign dug into the earth. It said "Tod für alle Juden". The congregation gathered around the building. Their eyes were glassed over. Dan saw tears running down the face of his own father. Dan's father translated the sign. It said "Death to the Jews." It did not occur to anyone huddled around the site that such hatred still existed in this modern world.

Dan tugged at his father's pant leg and asked for his knife. Dan's father reached into his pocket, pulled it out and gave it to him, not knowing why. Dan took the knife, walked up to the burnt out doorframe and carefully pried off the mezuzah. He took a rag from the ground, still wet from the fireman's water hoses, and polished off the metal cover. He looked within and saw that the parchment was still intact.

Dan walked over to an adjacent park. The congregation noticed what was happening and followed, curious as to what the small boy was doing. Dan went to one of the trees, picked up a rock and drove the nails holding the mezuzah into the bark. The rabbi smiled, took a kipa from his pocket and placed it on his head. Together they began to recite the morning prayers. The congregation slowly joined in. Dan's father still had tears streaming down his face, but they were of a different sort.

The mayor and town council convened an emergency session. They would not stand by and let such a despicable act impact their town. An unused building was donated to the congregation, free of charge. The entire town was solicited for donations to purchase a new ark and Torah scroll. The new building would be opened within a week. The rabbi asked if Dan and his family would be so kind as to stay for the inauguration. They agreed.

That next Shabbat the entire congregation and it seemed as if the entire city, gathered in the park. The rabbi and Dan went up to the now familiar tree and carefully pried off the mezuzah. As the congregants held lit menorahs, the whole group walked as if in a processional, to the new building.

On reaching the new synagogue, Dan placed the mezuzah on the doorframe, wiped it cleaned with a cloth, touched it with his hand, moved his hand to his lips, kissed his fingers lightly, and walked into the new building. The congregants and townspeople did the same. Together, the town prayed for a world of peace for all. Dan and his family were made honorary residents and received a gift as lifelong members in the congregation.

When they returned home a package had been delivered for Dan. It was from the congregation. Inside the package was a replica of the synagogue's mezuzah. A short note was attached simply saying thank you and shalom.

Midrash Eikev
A Stiff Neck

Jeremiah had a most unfortunate accident when he was in the war that left his legs paralyzed. He could move his arms and hands but could not move his head. Jeremiah was confined to a wheelchair with a brace on his neck forcing him to look forward.

As time moved on, Jeremiah's life took on a type of rigidity that reflected his physical limitations. His daily routine was predictable and monotonous. He always woke at seven in the morning and went to bed at eleven in the evening, regardless of the day.

Weekdays he went to work at a widget factory, doing a monotonous job, 9:00 am to 5:00 pm. He did not talk with his fellow workers, nor did he vary his routine in any way. He showed up for work, did his job and went home. Even the widgets were plain, simple and a solid dull gray color. On weekends he just sat in his apartment, looking out of a large front room window at the street in front of his house.

All his meals were the same. He ate one piece of bread, one small piece of meat, one vegetable and tea. Jeremiah wanted firmness and simplicity. The meal provided what nutrition he required and that was all that mattered. No variation and no additions were ever made to his diet.

Jeremiah had no friends, no acquaintances, and no relatives that he spoke with. His phone never rang and he never socialized. He kept to himself as much as he could and only communicated with others when he had to. He withdrew into himself and set up as many barriers to the outside as possible. It was lonely, but Jeremiah felt comfort in his segregated life.

The widget factory was sold. The new owners visited and inspected each of the stations that were involved in the production. They got to Jeremiah's station and began to ask questions. He responded that he had always done this job the same way and demonstrated his technique. The owners said that they were looking to upgrade the factory and to expect some changes in the near future.

Over the next week everything pretty much stayed the same. Jeremiah still showed up for his job and did his part on the production line. Then one day different colored widgets began to appear. The old gray widgets had suddenly become blue, red and green. A variety of colored widgets made their way down the production line. This stunned Jeremiah.

The owners said that although the factory would continue to work, construction crews would begin to expand different sections of the production line. Workers suddenly appeared from all directions and an organized chaos erupted throughout the plant.

As the week proceeded Jeremiah could see workers not only across different parts of the floor but overhead in cranes and below the floor in pits. His nerves frayed, Jeremiah used all his strength to maintain his semblance of routine.

Jeremiah was about to take his lunch break and rolled his wheelchair down an aisle toward the cafeteria. Out of the corner of his eye he saw an overhead cable break releasing a steel beam it was holding that was part of the new construction. It crashed down on the machine below. The feed conveyor to the machine on the floor snapped and shifted, catching the pant leg of the adjacent worker. The worker was swept up onto the conveyor and headed for a series of blades designed to cut the widgets. If he entered that section it most certainly would kill him.

Jeremiah twisted his chair and ran it into one of the side sprockets that controlled the conveyor leading to the blades. The twisting action of the sprockets slung Jeremiah out of his chair into the aisle way. The chair jammed into the mechanized parts and forced the machine to come to a halt.

238

Workers helped the man off the conveyor. He was not hurt, as the machine stopped just short of contacting him with the blades. Others helped prop Jeremiah against a building column. They could not put him into his wheelchair as the machine had mangled it.

The owners rushed to the area and asked what happened. Others reported what they saw. Oddly, the other workers did not know Jeremiah's name. They knew he worked one of the stations but because nobody talked with him, they did not know who he was. Jeremiah flushed with embarrassment. The owners thanked him and asked for his name. "Jeremiah", he said. The owners lifted their voice to the assembled crowd and publicly thanked Jeremiah for his help in saving the other worker.

Jeremiah was taken home. He had another wheelchair there, although the factory owners said they would have a new one delivered to him. Jeremiah thought about the activities of the day. His action did not seem heroic or anything special. He saw what needed to be done and did it. Yet the interplay with others brought back fond memories of times before the war. It exhilarated him. His former life seemed cold and isolated. He vowed to try and change.

The new wheelchair was given to Jeremiah at a factory ceremony. It contained all the various colors the new widgets came in. The co-workers now took the time to talk with Jeremiah and he made an effort to talk with them. A new kind of social activity erupted at the cafeteria. People would bring and trade homemade delicacies for others to try. Jeremiah soon found his diet expanded and the tastes made his whole body smile.

A new computer program was installed at Jeremiah's station. In the old days he assumed the computer was there to replace him. In fact it made his job much easier and allowed the plant to produce many more widgets. Jeremiah could not change his outward physical limitations but he no longer felt that the outside had to reflect what was within.

Midrash Re'eh
A Small Suggestion

Steven was invited to a small class to speak about
Judaism. The school was in the heart of the big city. As he
drove to the talk he passed dirty streets, bordered up houses
and just an overall depressed neighborhood. This part of the
city was poor and it reflected on the faces he passed.

The students in this particular school were Christian and Muslim. They knew nothing about Judaism. Steven talked to the students about the basic beliefs of his religion and how Jews applied them. He taught a little Hebrew and answered many questions. They sang and laughed and learned.

Toward the end of the talk Steven passed a Tzedakah Box around to the students. He asked them to place any spare money they had into the container. The students thought that Steven would keep the money as payment for his talk. He opened the box and counted the change. He then reached into his own pocket and matched what was in the box.

Steven said that one of the main beliefs in Judaism is charity. He explained that the word Tzedakah is Hebrew for charity. The students, though poor, could still help others. It was not the amount that counted but the effort put forth. The students asked if the money should go to a Jewish charity. Steven said any good cause would make it a mitzvah, a good deed. He said that the students could look at life as a blessing or a curse. He understood that their lives were hard but they could still look at life in a positive way and strive to help others.

Steven asked the students to collect money daily. The students should never give more than they can, never in a way that would hurt themselves or their families. A few months from now they could decide for themselves which cause needed the money and give it to them. It did not have to be a religious organization, just any group that the students felt needed it. The students seemed excited about the project and agreed to do it.

The students in the class talked to others throughout the school. They talked about what they learned and about the project. Soon other classes decided to join in and then the entire school. After a few months they had collected a large sum of money. The students began to talk about who should receive the money. The teachers used the project to present what different charitable organizations did around the world.

The whole school met in the auditorium to talk about which group to give the money to. There were many arguments and some suggested that they should split the money and give to a number of different groups. Then a little girl asked to go onstage to speak to the school. In her small voice she suggested that they take the money and use it for their own neighborhood. To clean up the streets, plant trees, bushes and flowers. We should make our own neighborhood a nicer place. The students loved the idea and voted unanimously to accept it.

The school invited the mayor to visit. They presented him the money they collected and asked him to use it to help fix up the neighborhood. Television cameras showed the presentation to the whole city. The mayor said that he was so proud of what the students did that the city council would also give money to the effort.

Over the next few weeks the streets in the neighborhood were transformed. Others came forward to lend support. Contactors, residents and friends volunteered their time and money. Dirty dingy streets became clean, pretty and welcoming. As the streets were transformed physically, the frame of mind of the residents seemed to change as well. Families would go out at night to meet and talk with their neighbors. Children, before confined indoors because of the unsafe conditions, now played together outside.

What started out as a small suggestion to a single class had grown to encompass the entire city. The combination of a little charity and a new attitude had transformed this little corner of the world into a vibrant community.

Midrash Shoftim
The Copy

Daniel was a biochemist at a large pharmaceutical company. The company had a policy that required a small percentage of their work time to be devoted to charitable projects.

Daniel chose to concentrate on finding the cause and cure for an ailment that affected only about one hundred people nationwide annually. Because it affected so few people it was unlikely that any company would put forth effort to find a cure. It simply was not economical. The government would not fund any effort for the same reason. Daniel decided to make it his charity project.

The disease had a very unusual side affect. When it first manifested itself the person affected would go through a cycle of personal plagues. First blood blisters would cover their body. This was followed by the skin turning a frog-like green, followed by little white growths that looked like lice, followed by boils erupting over the infected person's body. Lastly the skin turned an ashen color that made the person look like a corpse. Each plague would last no more than one week and then disappear. There would be a few days rest and the next plague appeared. The worst part was that within one year of the last plague, the person died.

Daniel had many responsibilities at the company and could set aside only about ten hours a week for the project. As a biochemist Daniel's main focus was on the chemicals found within the human body. He isolated thousands of compounds and then tested the blood donated by a few of the affected people to see if it was present. Test after test, compound after compound, year after year, Daniel's effort resulted in one dead end after another. Then he discovered an enzyme that seemed absent from those who contracted the disease. He tested a number of samples from different victims and it was always lacking in that enzyme. He did not know how the lack of this compound caused the plagues and death of those that did not produce it, only that they seem to lack it.

Now that the enzyme was isolated, the question moved to how to replicate it. It was a very complicated organic compound. He tried time and again to produce it within his laboratory but never could get it just right. With dogged perseverance he finally reproduced the complex molecule.

He now had to test it. The enzyme was specific to humans. Other animals did not have this compound in their bodies nor was he aware of any mention of other animals having this ailment. He could prove it was not harmful when ingested by animals, which was an FDA requirement, but could not tell what it would do with human beings or for that matter if replacing the enzyme would help at all. It was simply an educated guess. The FDA gave Daniel the go ahead to try it on a few patients, if he could get their approval. As it was not something that would be mass distributed they did not have much concern.

Daniel contacted those who recently showed the signs of the plagues. All who were contacted said they would act as part of the test group as they knew the end result of the disease. Daniel chose twelve from the group. The pharmaceutical company agreed to transport the individuals to the local hospital where the drug would be administered and pick up the costs of the hospital stay.

Daniel had a close associate at a rival pharmaceutical company. It was a friend he grew up with and went to the same college. They maintained contact after graduation, even though they ended up in rival companies. For safe keeping Daniel decided to send a copy of his work to his friend. He asked him to keep it confidential but wanted it in a second location. His friend agreed.

The day before the test a fire broke out at the building where Daniel worked. The fire spread quickly. Explosions could be heard at various intervals, destroying whole parts of the building. Daniel, his papers and the manufactured enzymes were all caught in one of those explosions and were destroyed.

A few days later the hospital board met to arrange for the test patients to be returned to their homes. Daniel's friend interrupted the meeting and said he had a copy of Daniel's work and if they would give him a few days he would make up the enzyme samples to allow the test to go forward. Although the Company upset that Daniel had sent copies of his research to a rival, the hospital agreed to allow the test to move forward. The test did go on and was a full success. The patients not only recovered but lived a full long life. Others affected by the disease were also given the enzyme and cured. The carriers of this disease decided to stay in communication with each other and formed an association. The charter group numbered less than eighty people, including the original twelve.

The Association wanted to provide some kind of memorial for Daniel. The discussion between the members lasted for almost a year. Suggestions ranged from renaming a hospital in his name, to naming the drug after him, to placing a wall up somewhere in his dedication. None seem to do justice to his contribution.

One of the communiqués from a member said that he was so thankful to Daniel that he and his wife decided to use Daniel as the middle name of their newborn son. Word quickly spread to the other members who embraced the idea.

It was decided by unanimous vote of the members, that from this point forward any new baby born by an association member would carry the middle name of Daniel for a boy or Danielle for a girl. This memorial was to celebrate life for one who helped give life.

As time went by the children of these association members began to have families of their own. They decided to keep the tradition when naming their own babies and future generations would be asked to also keep this tradition. A few hundred years elapsed. The Association decided to hold a reunion in New York City. People from all over the world attended. There were over ten thousand people at that party. All had the middle name of Daniel or Danielle.

Midrash Ki Teitzei
Lost and Found

John worked at the city's summer amusement park. It wasn't anything exciting but he made a few dollars and could stay outside in the nice weather until the fall, when school would start again.

At the end of a shift he noticed a shiny sparkle of something under one of the picnic tables. John walked over for a closer inspection. It was a piece of jewelry. The end of the piece could be seen just outside a velvet bag and caught the sun's rays enough to allow John to see the glittering object.

John opened the bag and removed its contents. It was a diamond-studded necklace. It shined like something he had never seen before. Looking around, the park was deserted. John had no thought of keeping the bobble himself. He wanted to return the necklace to the rightful owner.

Checking with the park's administration, he learned that only one group had reserved that particular table for the day. It was a group of older ladies that had formed their own club and toured different places around the city. The park gave John a copy of the attendees. He resolved to go the next day and visit those on the list to see if he could find the owner of the necklace.

John started first thing the next morning and walked up a small set of stairs to the front door of his first inquiry. An older gentleman answered the door. He looked tired. His eyes were red and swollen, as if he had been crying for some time. John asked if Sally, whose name he got from the list, was home. My name is Julius and Sally is my wife. Julius explained that Sally collapsed last night and was in bed. The doctor said that cancer had spread throughout her body. She can no longer walk and will not live much longer. Sally's excursion yesterday was her last time out of the house.

John asked if he could see Sally. Julius said that it was all right but she was not too coherent because the doctor had given Sally a good deal of medicine to help numb the pain. John went into the room where Sally was laying in a large expansive bed. He tried to explain a little about the lost piece of jewelry. Sally, in slight delirium, said she recognized the boy as her long lost brother! Julius said not to worry, it was the drugs, and she really did not know what she was saying. Julius asked if John would just play along.

John took a seat near the bed and talked with Sally. She noticed the velvet bag and asked what was in it. John pulled out the necklace. She screamed in delight- "My Necklace! Please give it to me so I may put it on." Julius whispered in John's ear. He said she did not own any such piece of jewelry and again asked for him to play along.

John complied and handed the necklace to Julius. He strung it around his wife's neck. The jewelry looked surreal against the flannel nightgown. Sally said to give John a reward for finding her jewelry. Julius reached into his pocket and handed John a $100 bill.

The three of them continued to talk the day away. Sally rambled endlessly about growing up and kept telling different stories about the experiences of her life. John enjoyed listening about the different people and different places. As Sally talked she fondled the necklace and gestured in a most extravagant manner. The smile on her face was wide, large and infectious.

They talked a little longer and Sally fell asleep. Julius carefully took off the necklace and both he and John exited the room. As Julius escorted John out, he handed him back the necklace. John went to hand the $100 bill back and the husband told him to please keep it for being so kind to his wife. Julius said that he knew whom the necklace belonged to and pointed out the name on the list that John got from the Park. John thanked him and left.

John went to the house of the real owner. The owner described the necklace before John could even ask. John handed the bag over. The owner opened the bag and slipped out the necklace, admiring its beauty. She said this piece had been in her family for many generations, it was an heirloom. In her old age she was getting forgetful and intended to give the necklace to her daughter. As she went to put the necklace back into the bag she felt the rustle of a piece of paper within. She reached into the bag and pulled out the $100 bill.

She turned to John and inquired, as she knew that she did not place any money into the bag. John said that the necklace had earned the $100 and that since she was the owner of the necklace that he would like her to have it. The lady seemed very confused by the statement and placed the bill back into the velvet bag. She profusely thanked John for his kindness in returning the family heirloom.

John's thought of Sally often. The necklace looked so funny against her old flannel nightgown and of the way her eyes shined beautifully when her husband placed it on her neck. He would often think of her smile, and every time a smile would appear on his face as well.

Midrash Ki Tavo
A Mitzvah of Action

Christopher and David served on the city council.
Both were elected at the same time and currently began serving
a second term of office. Christopher was president of the
council and David a member from one of the districts.

The city was large and in decent shape. Finances were stable and there were no great issues that needed immediate attention. Times were good and the council meetings were upbeat and friendly. At one meeting however, a lady stood up in the back of the hall and said that there was a section of town in need of a great deal of help. They were poor and most did not have jobs. The schools were in disrepair and she felt the city and this council should do something about it.

Christopher rose out of his chair and in a magnanimous voice thanked the lady and said that the council would look into the matter immediately, at which time he went on with other business.

A month later the same lady showed up at the council meeting and asked what had been done. Christopher rose again from his chair and said that the executive board had discussed the matter and was in process of developing a plan.

A third month passed with the same exchange. David feeling uncomfortable with the situation decided to look into the matter. He asked the lady if she would agree to meet with him to show him her neighborhood and explain what the problem was. She agreed.

David could hardly believe his eyes. Crossing a railroad track at the east end of town moved him into a totally different world. The poverty was overwhelming. Houses were more like shacks, the streets were dirty, the playgrounds overgrown with weeds, and broken glass was everywhere. The lady said most of the residents were unemployed and though the rest of the city seemed to be just fine, this neighborhood was a forgotten place. They needed help.

The lady, frustrated and disillusioned, did not show up at the next meeting. During the council meeting David stood and asked Christopher what the executive council came up with as it related to the city's east end. Christopher made a wonderful speech and said that the council itself would split up into different work groups to come up with a plan. The residents in the audience seemed very pleased with the idea.

David had enough talk. He could not sit by and endlessly discuss the issue. The next day he went to his close friend at the lumber yard and explained the situation. He asked him to donate some materials to help out. Next, David gathered a few friends, a few trucks and whatever tools he could muster and drove to the lady's house. He pulled up and honked the horn. She appeared and David asked where they should start.

That was the first of many days David and other city residents spent on the other side of the tracks. As they worked, they trained local residents how to do various chores. They learned carpentry, plumbing, general construction, and a host of other skills that not only assisted in repairing the area but helped these newly skilled workers find work with different companies. Those that found jobs always returned the favor and spent many days themselves in rebuilding the neighborhood. The action was contagious. More people hearing of the success donated their time cleaning, constructing and teaching.

Over time, the other side of the tracks became a pretty nice place to live. During those same months Christopher and the council continued to talk about what to do and marveled at how their talking resulted in turning the neighborhood on the other side of tracks around. They even had plaques made in their honor. David took his, ripped off the brass emblem on the front and used the wood backing for a repair job.

Midrash Nitzavim
A Far Away Search

Gabriel had just turned 18. He graduated High School and in a few months would start college. Gabriel grew up in a stable Jewish home. His relationship with his parents and siblings were good. As a youngster he attended religious school and had a Bar Mitzvah at age 13. His family celebrated all the Jewish holidays, yet were not an overtly religious family. They belonged to a synagogue but rarely attended. They supported many Jewish causes financially, but did not really involve themselves.

Gabriel was comfortable in his existence but there was something missing. He could not quite put a finger on it. Nothing seemed out of place or not in order. Yet he felt emptiness, a void that unnerved him, that caused him to worry. It manifested itself in shpilkes- a Yiddish word meaning restless anxiety, nervous energy – a word whose pronunciation perhaps describes the condition better than the definition.

Gabriel had saved a good amount of money over the years and he had been able to secure a scholarship for college, so he would not have to dip into his savings. He decided to spend some of those funds on summer travel. His parents had no objection. He decided to not just travel aimlessly but to pick one locale as different as possible from what he was used to: Japan.

It could not be a big city, like Kyoto or Tokyo, as that would have too many similarities to home. Gabriel decided on a small village near Mt. Fuji called Oshino. Gabriel's father had a Japanese friend who was able to set up a place for Gabriel to stay in that village. It was a local residence of an elderly couple that had known the friend when he was a boy. They would make Gabriel welcomed.

As Gabriel set off for the airport a small twinge shook his body. Something deep within welled up and spewed forth a prayer, a blessing he had learned long ago. It was a Jewish prayer said at the start of a trip. He could not remember the Hebrew but did remember the English translation. "May it be Your will, LORD, our God and the God of our ancestors, that You lead us toward peace, guide our footsteps toward peace, and make us reach our desired destination for life, gladness, and peace."

Travel to Oshino encompassed all forms of transportation. Planes from the United States to Japan, trains to get as close to the village as possible, followed by vans and then finally with his own feet he walked to the village. With each form of locomotion Gabriel seemed to be transported back in history.

The village was small and quaint. It did not take long to find the residence where he would be staying. When greeted at the house he was motioned to remove his shoes. The hosts did not speak English. They motioned for Gabriel to don some house slippers that were adjacent to the door. Gabriel slid across the hard wood floors to the next room. In the center was a heated table looking structure. Although summer, it was still cool in these mountains at night and his hosts showed him how to use a comforter and the heated table to stay warm and cozy in the evening.

On rising in the morning, Gabriel looked out a veranda to a majestic view of Mt. Fuji filling the sky. He decided to take a walk through the village. It was not long until he reached the end of this tiny community. For as far as his eyes could see, sunflowers, tall in stature with yellow petal heads, stretching up to frame the mountain in the background. He began walking through these fields and nature enveloped his very existence. From the depths of his soul he felt that same twinge from the beginning of this journey. Without understanding how or even why he began to sing a prayer he had learned long ago in religious school- the Shehecheyanu. "Blessed are You, LORD, our God, King of the universe, Who has kept us alive, sustained us, and enabled us to reach this season."

A few days passed and his hosts had been most kind. Gabriel decided to visit a Shinto shrine. Japan is the home to the Shinto religion. A foundational precept in this religious outlook is the creative force of nature and the nature around this village was breathtaking.

He traveled by foot toward the mountains. A Sengen shrine greeted Gabriel. The main building was modest and unimpressive. There was a gate leading to a trail that led half-way up the mountain. The trail contained a forest of tall cedar trees, and coupled with the majestic mountain vistas, took Gabriel's spirit and raised it to a heavenly level.

Along the trail, Gabriel stopped to talk with a Shinto priest who was resting on the side of the road. The priest knew English. He explained, "Shinto means the Way of the Gods and can be traced as far back as 500 BCE. Shinto Gods and the Gods of the West are not similar in any way. The Shinto Gods, or Kami, are related to nature and creative forces. It is our hope to obtain makoto, a true heart, in harmony with and through nature. This is why our shrines are in places like this." The two continued to talk for a while longer. Gabriel felt it was time to move on and thanked the priest for helping him understand their way.

Gabriel moved to a secluded spot on the mountain and sat to absorb all that was around him; the majesty, the beauty, and the life that embodied this spot. Harmony filled his body. At first Gabriel thought he was feeling the Shinto way. A twinge from deep within and once again a Jewish prayer floated forth. "Blessed are You, LORD, our God, King of the Universe, Who bestows good things on the unworthy, and has bestowed on me every goodness." He remembered that this was a prayer for illness or danger, but the words seemed so perfect for what he was feeling at that moment. Gabriel rose, took one last appreciative glance at this mountain, and moved on.

On his return to the host family, they prepared a wonderful meal for Gabriel. They made a dish of soba buckwheat noodles, a local dish from grains grown just outside the village. The food was a texture that he had never experienced before. It was so light and delicious. Once again the twinge, and once again a Jewish prayer, this time uttered aloud; "Blessed are You, LORD, our God, King of the universe, Who brings forth bread from the earth." On hearing this strange language the host couple seemed bewildered and confused. Gabriel smiled, bowed politely, and thanked them in their native tongue for this wonderful food.

At summer's end Gabriel returned home. In Oshino he learned about the Shinto religion, but it was not Shinto that resonated with his essence. It was Judaism. It wasn't that he had to cross the seas and travel to a distant land to find this out. It was actually very near. It was within him. It was part of him. With this understanding, the shpilkes , the void, disappeared. As he entered his home, one more Jewish prayer rose from deep inside. It was the Modeh Ani, the prayer said when a person wakes up in the morning. "I give thanks before You, Living and Eternal King, that You have returned within me my soul with compassion; how abundant is Your faithfulness!"

Midrash Vayelech
The Passing of the Torch

There was a strong tradition in Mike's family that went back three generations. His great grandfather immigrated to the United States from Russia as a young boy and became a successful businessman in this country of opportunity. He built a factory that specialized in the assembly of small parts. At first he hired other Russian immigrants to staff the factory. Mike's grandfather, after receiving his education, went to work in the factory and eventually took over running the plant when his great grandfather retired.

Mike's grandfather continued the successful plant. His largest problem was that the immigrants began to leave the plant after they accumulated enough money to go off on their own. The "Great War" had started in Europe. Many of the able men went into the military and there was a real shortage of able workers. Mike's grandfather came up with the idea of hiring women. They needed money to help support their families while their husbands were away fighting the war. It turns out that the women did a very nice job, thank you, and it also turns out that there was more than one "Great War". Mike's father, like his grandfather, grew up around the plant and worked there after he finished school. He too, when the time was right, took over the running of the plant.

Mike's father continued the successful plant. His largest problem was that many of the women left the plant after their husbands returned from the wars. There were not enough new women to staff the plant. Mike's father began hiring Russian immigrants, like his great grandfather did. There were not enough, so he hired any immigrant that wanted a job. Often they would come in as an ethnic group and he would hire them all. The group he hired might be from any part of the world. It was strange to walk through the factory. Chinese, Africans, Pakistanis and people from every part of the globe filled the plant. Walking through the factory, depending on where you were, different languages were heard, different foods could be smelled that were brought in for their breaks, and clothes from every part of the globe could be seen. As different as these people were culturally, they worked side by side with each other and the plant ran very well.

Mike, like his grandfather, grew up around the plant and worked there after school. He too, when the time was right, took over the running of the plant.

Mike continued the successful plant. The largest problem was that many of the immigrants began to leave the plant after they made enough money to go off on their own. There did not seem to be enough immigrants to hire.

Mike was a strong believer in giving back to the community. He was involved in a number of charitable causes. One day he was asked to help arrange for reconstruction at a hospital at the edge of town. He went to visit the establishment to get a better idea for what was needed. He found that the building was not a hospital in any sense he knew but a housing development for people with special needs. These were people who were limited intellectually or emotionally. Seeing people in such a state first repulsed Mike but then scared him.

He followed through on the promise he made to reconstruct the facility and spent more and more time at the hospital making sure the work was done properly. The more time he spent, the more he began to understand the differences in the people who lived in this hospital. Many were so limited as to be helpless. But there were a number that were aware and always in motion, doing something, especially with their hands.

Mike had a thought. He asked the hospital administrator if he could bring a few of the patients to the factory, with the hospitals assistance, to see if they would be able to do some of the jobs that were needed. The administrators found the idea intriguing and agreed.

It turns out that if a special needs person could not do a task immediately they would never be able to learn that job. However, if they did learn the task, they would do it very well. Mike made a contract with the hospital to employ any of the patients that could learn to do one of the jobs the plant needed. He would pay the workers a fair wage and also employ hospital staff to help at the factory.

These employees almost never missed a day of work. They were competent, committed and most of all, happy. The wages made them self-supportive and allowed the hospital to offer services that under normal circumstances could never have existed.

Mike's son spent his free time at the factory working alongside these new employees. Mike knew that one day he too would pass the factory on to his son. His son would face problems but would find a way to make the factory successful.

Parashat Haazinu
The Song

    Daniel lived in the Jewish quarter of a small village in Hungary with his mother, father and baby sister. He had just turned fourteen. World War II had spread throughout Europe and was heading for their country. The venom of anti-Semitism spread well in front of the Nazi armies and even their remote location seemed quarantined from their Gentile neighbors.

The family had just sat down to their Sabbath meal when they heard the rumble of military engines. Daniel's father told him to run and hide in the woods. He was not to say a word no matter what he saw or heard. His father kissed him on the forehead and again said, "Do not say a word."

Without hesitation Daniel did as his father told. As he ran to a grove of woods about fifty yards in back of their house, he turned and saw his father and mother. His mother was holding his baby sister, only a few months old, wrapped in a blanket, a forlorn expression on his mother's face. As a boy he had built a play fort. It was not much more than a hole in the ground nestled under some fallen trees, but he could hide by covering the hole over with vegetation. This type of covering allowed him to look out but no-one could look in.

Daniel could see a whole convoy of trucks roll into the village. The soldiers jumped out of the vehicles and scurried about. They moved in small bands and searched house to house, looking for any residents. Without the slightest hesitation they shot anyone they found.

Daniel saw the Nazis as they broke down the door of their house and dragged his father, mother and baby sister out. They placed them against the wall. A soldier, walking as if he was on a stroll through the park, meandered by his family and shot them dead. Daniel did not move from his hiding place or utter a sound as he saw his family drop to the ground like limp rags.

The Nazis left the dead lying on the ground as they went to search for other victims. Villagers who saw what was happening ran for the woods. Most were shot before they got even half way. A troop of soldiers combed the woods for survivors. Daniel fluffed the fort covering so that no light would penetrate. Through the remainder of the night he heard terrifying screams, always followed by gunfire and then silence. The screams made Daniel's skin crawl. But he did not utter a sound. He would follow his father's instructions.

It was well into the next day before Daniel crawled out of his hiding place. He went back to his house and buried his family. Although tears filled his eyes and poured down his cheeks, Daniel uttered no sound. He went to the broken doorframe and with a small knife pried the mezuzah off the wood jam. He slipped it through a small chain and placed it around his neck, letting it hang by his heart, inside his shirt. He returned to the woods to spend another night in his fort, hiding from any soldiers who may have continued to search.

The next day Daniel traveled away from the village. He took care to avoid the German soldiers. He walked for days and kept as hidden as possible. He ran into a troop of freedom fighters also hiding in the woods. When the leader of the troop questioned Daniel he noticed that he used the fewest words possible to communicate. If Daniel could he would answer with a gesture and never a sound.

Daniel joined the small band and learned to shoot Nazis using guerrilla tactics. The small troop would hit when and where they could, and then slip back into the woods. In short order Daniel became the fiercest fighter the troop had. Whenever they were in a battle Daniel killed more Nazis than three other freedom fighters put together, and in the process never uttered a word.

The small band respected Daniel but did not quite know how to take him. They thought him crazy. It wasn't the fact that he did not speak but even when fighting he showed no emotion. His face was like a stone. He shot and moved, shot and moved- almost mechanical. His technique was perfect and as smooth a fighter as they had ever seen. He never mourned, never cried, never smiled, never spoke.

For years the war dragged on, and then it ended. The Nazis had been beaten. The freedom fighters were disbanding and going home. But Daniel did not know where home was. He would not return to the village. He decided to go to Palestine. He heard that Jews were settling there and that they needed fighters. He did not know a trade other than fighting. He might find work there.

The British were not allowing any new immigration into Palestine and had closed the border. That was no problem for Daniel. He used his skills to sneak into the country. Quickly he found other Jewish fighters clawing out a position here or there, either against the ruling British or the local contingent of Arabs. He fit well into the small Israeli fighter bands. His quiet unemotional ways were as much an asset in the crowded streets of Jerusalem as they were in the forests of Hungary.

The British mandate was about to end. It was November 29, 1947 and a crowd of Jews, including Daniel, filled a square near the Tel Aviv Museum. Ben-Gurion and his associates came out onto the balcony of the building and gave the crowd updates on the United Nations vote for Israeli statehood. Daniel could feel the electrical ebb and flow in the mass of people around him.

When the final vote was tallied, statehood was granted. Israel was to be a nation. The crowd screamed in jubilation. Daniel did not make a peep. The crowd suddenly got very quiet. Not a sound was heard through the square. Then, very low, almost imperceptibly, these new citizens began to sing the Hatikvah. Hatikvah means 'The Hope' and became the national anthem of Israel. Something began to well up deep inside Daniel. It was something he had never felt before. He began to sing with the crowd. As he sang, tears flowed down his face. It gushed as if a dam in a river had suddenly let loose. As the song progressed Daniel's notes got louder and louder.

When the song was done, big circles formed in the middle of the street. People joined hands, danced and sang. Daniel could not help himself. He coupled his hands with someone within the circle, sang out in unison with his fellow countrymen and danced. Daniel danced so hard that the mezuzah tucked in his shirt flew around his head like a twirling ribbon. He danced until he could dance no longer and collapsed in the street- smiling.

Israel was not only his country but also his family. He joined the regular army to help defend the newborn nation. He still fought as hard and as efficient as he always had. He still spoke rarely. But when he heard a song or saw a dance, it was as if some power overtook him. He would join in, sing and let his emotion pour out. Daniel was home.

Midrash Vezot
From Bereshit to Kol Israel and Back Again

Abe had a long career as a doctor but it was time for retirement. The daily grind and long hours had taken their toll over the years. He loved being a doctor but his body could no longer sustain the effort required.

After resting for a few months Abe wanted to try something new. He always wanted to sail around the world. It wasn't the idea of traveling to a particular port that appealed to him, but to go where the sea and wind moved him.

Abe bought a used boat and spent the next six months fixing it up. The one item he was most proud of was the captain's chair. He had it rigged so he could control any part of the ship from its perch. He even created a device that could rise into place during bad weather. It had see-through sides and a roof. When in position, coupled with the odd looking captain's chair, it looked like a giant Hebrew letter Bet. He had the ship renamed Bereshit, which also started with a Bet, as this was a new beginning for him, a new creation.

Abe spent the first year touring the Caribbean, going from Island to Island, and learning how to maneuver Bereshit in any type of weather. His proudest achievement was learning how to get the most out of the sails instead of using the motor. By year's end he knew his craft well.

It was time to embark on his world tour. Abe developed a method to his venture. He did not just pull into port and leave immediately for another spot on the globe. He stopped and spent time learning the local culture and beliefs. Although Abe grew up Jewish, he wanted to experience how others lived and felt.

Through his travels he noticed that there were certain foundational principals that all people followed. They may be called by different names, and may even be approached differently, but were the same core beliefs. One was hospitality, another, the sacredness of life. Even with rampant prejudice and xenophobia that permeated this world, there was an understanding of what was right or wrong.

Abe decided to spend some time around the Mediterranean. He slowly worked his way across the North African coastline. Upon entering a particularly small port, he was arrested and thrown into the local jail. This village had close ties with the Palestinians and noticed the name of the boat. They threw Abe in jail for being Jewish.

The tiny town was in turmoil, with fighting between different bands of rebels who raided the town. It was a scene of constant chaos and danger. In the last skirmish a boy had been badly wounded. The leadership of the town was worried, as the boy was the son of a key leader in the Palestinian government and they could find no doctor.

Rumor had reached the jail about the incident. One of Abe's cellmates told the local guard that Abe was a doctor and could help. The guard told the local magistrate who had Abe brought to the boy. The magistrate asked if Abe would help. Abe said he would. The magistrate told him the boy was Palestinian and the son of an important political opponent to Israel. Abe responded that he already knew this. The magistrate knew Abe was Jewish. "Why would you help this boy?" Abe turned and said, "Because it is the right thing to do".

274

A stray bullet had lodged near the boy's heart. Abe was able to remove it and stayed with him during the recovery for the next two weeks. Fighting with the rebels continued and shots were heard frequently in the streets. The magistrate was able to get word to the boy's father about the incident. His father wanted him to return home. The airport was closed and the roads were too dangerous to try. The magistrate asked Abe if he would use his boat to sail the boy home.

Abe agreed, as he really wanted to leave this place. At nightfall guards took the boy and Abe to the boat. Abe, the boy, and a few guards assigned to make the trip, boarded the boat and lifted the sails. Silently and slowly Bereshit drifted out of port.

National news reporters caught wind of the story as they were covering the rebel uprising. While Abe slowly made his way toward Israel, newspapers all over the world read about a Jewish doctor who saved a Palestinian boy in the middle of all the horror that is war.

A few days later the small ship pulled into a Gaza port. They were greeted by the boy's father, a small group of doctors, hundreds of news reporters, and thousands of people. The boy's father walked up a raised platform to speak to the crowd. He publicly thanked Abe for his help, grasped Abe by the shoulders and kissed him on both cheeks. He then turned to the crowd and asked his fellow Palestinians a favor. "For the next twenty-four hours let us do honor to this man for his unselfish deeds. Let there be not one bullet shot, not one person killed, not one act of violence against the Israelis or any Jew around the world by the hand of a Palestinian."

The Israeli Knesset heard the remarks and asked that all Israelis act in kind. Not one Israeli should fire a bullet or do any act of violence toward a Palestinian for the next day.

The miracle occurred. For twenty-four hours not one fatality was reported, not one bullet fired. Not even one disturbance was called in to the local police. For one day all of Israel, *Kol Yisrael,* and in fact all the Middle East had true Shalom, peace.

Abe returned to his ship. He would not wait another day to see if the peace would hold. Leaving at this time, the feeling of Shalom, would remain with him always. He thought back to the beginnings of his new life. It started with Bereshit, creation. It ended with Kol Yisrael, all the people of Israel. Abe returned to Bereshit again. Firm in his beliefs, he would see where his ship would take him next.

Glossary of Jewish Terms

Aliyah: The honor, accorded to a worshiper, of being called up to read an assigned passage from the Torah. The term itself is translated as "going up" and refers to the usual placement of a Torah scroll to be read on a bimah, a raised stage like structure or altar.

Bar or Bat Mitzvah: Term Bar Mitzvah translates as "son of the commandment" and Bat Mitzvah is "daughter of the commandment". It is a Jewish rite of passage celebrated around a child's thirteenth birthday commemorating entry into the Jewish community. It usually takes place during a Sabbath service, when the child reads from a Torah scroll and may give a speech on the text. Through the ceremony the child becomes an adult in the eyes of the community as it relates to religious responsibilities.

Ben-Gurion, David: In the 1920s and '30s David Ben-Gurion led several political organizations, including the Jewish Agency, world Zionism's highest directing body. As a key Zionist leader, David Ben-Gurion had the honor of declaring Israel an independent state in 1948. He served as Israel's first Prime Minister until he retired in 1953. Ben-Gurion returned to politics and served as Prime Minister from 1955 until he stepped down in 1963.

Bet: The second letter of the Hebrew alphabet. Hebrew is read from right to left. The letter looks as follows- ב

Bimah: A Hebrew term for a raised stage area in a synagogue where the Torah scroll is read and religious services are led.

Bissel: Yiddish term for "a little bit."

Brit: Hebrew word for covenant. A covenant is an agreement between parties. In Judaism the covenant is an agreement between humanity and God. It began with Abraham and was renewed by his son Isaac and then Abraham's grandson Jacob. The Brit/Covenant is an agreement passed on through all Jews, across all generations.

Brit Milah: A religious ceremony welcoming Jewish boys into a covenant, brit, between God and the Children of Israel through ritual circumcision. This happens on the eighth day of the child's life.

Bubbe: Yiddish term for grandmother

Chai: The Hebrew word for life

Challah: A special braided egg bread eaten by Jews on the Sabbath, holidays and special occasions.

Hatikvah: The Hebrew word translates as "The Hope". The poem, written by Naftali Herz Imber, became Israel's national anthem.

Havdalah: The Hebrew word means "separation". It is a prayer service composed of four blessings, done at sundown on Saturday night that formally ends the Jewish Sabbath and begins the weekdays.

Jerusalem Stones: The special limestone quarried from the hills surrounding Jerusalem. It is a white stone used to build many of the structures in the Old city of Jerusalem, both in ancient and modern times.

278

Kavanah: The word can mean concentration, intent or feelings of the heart. It is a Hebrew term that includes the meaning behind an action.

Knesset: The legislative branch of the Israeli government. It can also mean the building that this body meets in.

Kipa: A skullcap worn by Jewish men and boys, and sometimes Jewish women. Orthodox men wear them at all times, other denominations will wear them only during prayer services. The Hebrew word means "dome". The Yiddish term for this item is "yarmulke".

Kohen Gadol: The title of High Priest of early Israelite religion until the destruction of the Second Temple of Jerusalem. The high priests belonged to the family line of Aaron, the first High Priest.

Kosher: The Hebrew word translates as "fit". It refers to the selection, slaughtering procedures and preparation of foods in accordance with traditional Jewish ritual and dietary laws.

Lecha Dodi: Hebrew words meaning "Come, my beloved". It is a poem and song composed by Shelomoh ha-Levi in the 16th-century. It is used in many Jewish Friday night Sabbath services as a welcoming to the Sabbath.

Manna: The food miraculously supplied to the Israelites during their 40 years of wanderings in the wilderness, as described in Exodus 16:14-35.

Matzah: Unleavened bread made from dough which is completely free of yeast or leavening and which is baked before the onset of fermentation. It is eaten by Jewish people during the festival of Passover.

Menorah/Hanukiah: The menorah is a seven branched candelabra used in the ancient Temple in Jerusalem, a symbol of Judaism since ancient times and the emblem of the modern state of Israel. The Hanukiah is nine-branched candelabra used during the Jewish festival of Hanukkah.

Mensch: A Yiddish term meaning an honorable, decent person, or an otherwise authentic person, a person who helps those who need help. The term can apply to a man, woman or child.

Mezuzah: A Hebrew term that means "doorpost". In modern times it is a decorative container marked with the symbol or word Shaddai, one of the Jewish names for God. It is placed on the doorposts of Jewish houses and contains a small parchment inscribed with the biblical passages Deuteronomy 6:4-9 and 11:13-21.

Mitzvah (sg)/Mitzvot (pl): Hebrew word meaning "commandment" or "good deed. In Judaism it refers to the 613 commandments given in the Torah. The term has also come to express an act of human kindness and/or moral laws.

Nazir: A Jewish person who dedicates himself to God for a small specified period of time by remaining in a state of purity for the duration of the vow. The vow was voluntarily taken for a period of about thirty days. During this time, the Nazirite was forbidden to drink or enjoy any product of the grape vine or other intoxicating beverages, to cut his hair, or to approach a dead body. The purpose of this vow was to allow a person to experience life as a ritually pure priest for a short period of time.

Nechdah: Hebrew word for granddaughter.

280

Parasha: Hebrew term meaning "portion". The Jewish Five Books of Moses are divided into 54 segments. Each segment is called a Parasha. In general, one Parasha is read for each calendar week out of a Torah scroll and is defined for that week worldwide.

Passover: A holiday beginning on the 14th of the Hebrew month of Nisan and celebrated for seven or eight days. The holiday commemorates the liberation of the Hebrew people from slavery in Egypt. It is one of the three pilgrimage holidays and is described in the Five Books of Moses.

Saba: Hebrew word for grandfather

Shabbat: Hebrew word meaning "rest". It begins for Jewish people at sundown on Friday and ends at sundown on Saturday. Shabbat refers to the Biblical account of creation in Genesis, describing God creating the Heavens and the Earth in six days, and resting on and sanctifying the seventh (Genesis 1:1-2:3). Traditionally, Shabbat is considered a festive day, when a person is freed from the regular labors of everyday life, can contemplate the spiritual aspects of life and can spend time with family.

Shalom: Hebrew word that can mean "hello", "goodbye" and/or "peace".

Shpilkes: Yiddish term for "nervous energy"

Simchat Torah: Hebrew term meaning "rejoicing with the Torah". It is a Jewish holiday celebrated on the 23rd of the Jewish lunar month of Tishri to celebrate the completion of the annual cycle of readings of the Torah

Tallit: A four-cornered, fringed prayer shawl worn during certain Jewish prayers, in fulfillment of the commandment of fringes (Numbers 15:38).

Talmud: The authoritative body of Jewish law and lore accumulated over a period of seven centuries (200 BCE-500 CE) both in Israel and Babylon. The word "Talmud" derives from the Hebrew root word *Lilamed* meaning "to study or teach". It is part of the Jewish Oral Law, traditionally given to Moses on Mount Sinai.

Tanach: A Hebrew acronym that forms the three sections of the written Torah or Bible. It is composed of the *Chumash* (Five Books of Moses), *Neviim* (Prophets) and *Ketuvim* (Writings).

Tikkun Olam: Hebrew term meaning "repair of the world". Term often used in the sense of a commitment to social action stemming from a Jewish outlook.

Torah Scroll: Also known as a *Sefer Torah*, it is a handwritten copy of the Five Books of Moses. It must meet extremely strict standards of production. The scroll is mainly used in the ritual of Torah reading during Jewish services. The scroll is handwritten in Hebrew on kosher parchment by a scribe.

Tzedakah: Hebrew word for "charity", based on the Hebrew word *tzedek* meaning "righteousness". In our modern day it refers to the collection of money for philanthropic activities, although in the broad sense it could mean any charitable activity.

Yad: A pointer used to help a reader keep his or her place when reading from a Torah scroll. Direct contact of the hands with the parchment of the scroll is forbidden as the oils or dirt from a person's skin can damage the parchment.

Yom Kippur: A holy and solemn day in the Jewish religious calendar. It is observed on the tenth of the Jewish lunar month of Tishri. Jewish people pray together as a community in the synagogue while observing a day long fast, from sunset when it commences until nightfall the next evening when it ends. Like the other major Jewish holidays, its authority derives from the Five Books of Moses, where it is called *Yom Ha-Kippurim,* "The Day of Atonement" (Leviticus 23:27, 32, 25:9).

Western Wall: The only modern remnant of the Jewish Second Temple in Jerusalem. The wall is actually part of a retaining wall outside the Temple itself. The Western Wall is now a site of pilgrimage, lamentation, and prayer by Jews and is sometimes called "The Wailing Wall". In Hebrew it is called *Ha-Kotel* and is built of large blocks of limestone cut for the Second Temple during the reign of Herod (37 - 4 B.C.E.).